D0027619

Hot and Bothered

erena Bell

Red-Hot Reads.

AVAILABLE THIS MONTH

#827 SEDUCING THE MARINE
Uniformly Hot!
Kate Hoffmann

#828 WOUND UP
Pleasure Before Business
Kelli Ireland

#829 HOT AND BOTHERED
Serena Bell

#830 AFTER MIDNIGHT
Holiday Heat
Katherine Garbera

ISBN-13: 978-0-373-79833-9

50550

EAN

"I don't want him to touch you..."

He'd said it without thought, without realizing what those words would feel like said out loud. How they would affect him—or her.

Mark watched the heat leaving Haven's face, her posture softening. She understood what he was trying to say to her: *I don't want anyone* but me *to touch you*.

She was staring at him. Her eyes were big, her lower lip soft and full, *begging* to be kissed, something uncertain in her stance. A hesitation he'd only noticed a few times before, those exposed moments in the mirror when he knew—*knew*—she was feeling the same pull he was. So unlike the woman Haven Hoyt presented to the world. So unlike the woman he knew she desperately wanted him and everyone else to see.

He acted on impulse, taking her mouth the way he'd wanted to so badly at the jam session, the way he'd wanted it staring at her reflection all day Saturday, the way he'd wanted it the first time he'd sat across from her in Charme. And she opened to him, pressing against him, all heat and spark.

Dear Reader,

Ever since Haven Hoyt made her grand entrance midway through *Still So Hot!* rolling her hot-pink patent-leather suitcase behind her, I've known she needed her own book. So I was delighted when the petite image consultant with the big personality hired *Still So Hot!*'s dating coach, Elisa, to find her the perfect guy.

Haven's idea of the perfect guy is someone just like her—polished, worldly and ready for prime-time viewing. But for some reason these guys *never* stick. Then Haven meets former pop star Mark Webster. On paper, Mark is all wrong for her—huffy, scruffy and a PR disaster waiting to happen. Plus, he's her client—it's Haven's job to clean up Mark's bad-boy image for an upcoming band reunion tour.

But Mark's got other ideas. He wants to teach Haven how to get messy. And before long, things between Haven and Mark are exactly that, complete with the jealous ex-bandmate who will stop at nothing to take away the things that matter most to Mark.

Welcome to a world of image, glitz, love and heart, a world where outside appearances matter, but what's inside matters more!

Love,

Serena

Serena Bell

Hot and Bothered

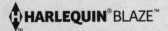

Recycling programs
for this product may
not exist in your area.

ISBN-13: 978-0-373-79833-9

Hot and Bothered

Copyright © 2015 by Serena Bell

This edition published by arrangement with Harlequin Books S.A.

For questions and comments about the quality of this book, please contact us at CustomerService@Harlequin.com.

HARLEQUIN®
™ www.Harlequin.com

Printed in U.S.A.

Serena Bell writes stories about how sex messes with your head, why smart people do stupid things sometimes and how love can make it all better. She wrote her first steamy romance before she was old enough to understand what all the words meant and has been perfecting the art of hiding pages and screens from curious eyes ever since—a skill that's particularly useful now that she's a mother of two avid readers. When she's not scribbling stories or getting her butt kicked at Scrabble by her kids, she's practicing modern dance improv in the kitchen, swimming laps, needlepointing, hiking or reading on one of her large collection of electronic devices. Serena blogs regularly about writing and reading romance at serenabell.com and wonkomance.com. She also Tweets like a madwoman as @serenabellbooks. You can reach her at serena@serenabell.com.

Books by Serena Bell

Harlequin Blaze

Still So Hot!

Visit the Author Profile page at
Harlequin.com for more titles

I've learned it takes a village to write a book. Huge thank-yous to my agent, Emily Sylvan Kim; my editor, Dana Hopkins; the Harlequin Blaze team; savvy readers Amber Belldene, Samantha Hunter, Ruthie Knox, Amber Lin, Mary Ann Rivers and Samantha Wayland; and indispensable morale boosters Rachel Grant, Lauren Layne, Ellen Price, Charlene Teglia, Mr. "Personal Shopper" Bell, the not-so-little-anymore MiniBells, my dad—who reads my books and loves them!—and, always, my amazing mom.

1

HAVEN HOYT SIPPED her water, smoothed her napkin over her lap and cast yet another glance toward the door of Charme, the see-and-be-seen Manhattan restaurant. Her newest client was late, but that didn't surprise her. Mark Webster had a reputation for being all *kinds* of unpredictable. Compared to some of the reasons his name had been splashed in the press, late to lunch was a minor sin.

She surveyed the restaurant again to make sure she hadn't missed him. She loved this place, with its half-circle booths like enormous club chairs and high ceilings baffled with great swoops of black and white. Light flooded the room through big front windows and from a million tiny halogens. She knew the restaurant's owner and its interior designer. And the publicist who had made it a sensation was a friend of Haven's—she *made* venues the way Haven *made* people.

Speaking of people Haven had made, Amanda Gile was dining with a well-known fashion writer two booths over, her adorable short haircut drawing attention to her high cheekbones and long neck. Haven smiled. A year ago, Amanda had opened a small boutique on Amsterdam. The New York fashion retail world had been ready to chew her up and spit her out, but Haven had transformed her into a celebutante—invited everywhere, fussed over, photographed. Haven had enjoyed every minute of the process—the shopping, the makeovers, the parties in the Hamptons where she'd draped her client over actors, producers, musicians and news makers. Amanda's success had boosted Haven's stock, too.

Mark Webster was going to be a lot more challenging than adorable, innocent Amanda Gile, but Haven had no doubt she could resuscitate his image. His pop group, Sliding Up, had taken high school girls by storm nine years ago, but now he was a has-been guitarist with a bad reputation. He boozed, he womanized, he brawled and he partied—and not in a slick, arm-around-an-*it*-girl way. He favored dark, sketchy clubs that he often managed to get himself tossed out of. And the sin that overrode all sins was that he put his foot in his mouth ninety percent of the time.

But as one of New York's premier image rehabilitators, Haven knew better than anyone that bad publicity was still publicity, and a star's light never went out.

The sound of a commotion at the door told Haven that Mark Webster had arrived. She'd done her homework, of course. She'd searched a million pictures of the guy online and couldn't help her tingle of interest at the fascinating contrast between his clean-cut boy-band self and the disaster he appeared to have become.

As a band member, he'd been golden and dimpled and damn cute. These days, his hair was too long to be sexy, his beard was a fungus trying to colonize his face, his eyes were often puffy and bloodshot, and he looked drunk in every photo.

Just like the guy who was leaning on the hostess stand now, an expression on his scruffy face that—on a less permanently pissed-off man—might have been pleading. But Mark looked sullen and faintly threatening. He was much bigger than Haven had guessed from the photos—tall, broad, built, undiminished by whatever hard living had taken the shine of youth off his features.

"I don't own a tie. Or a jacket. I'm meeting someone here, okay? She's over there." His voice was loud enough for Haven to hear now, his jaw thrust forward, his eyes narrow. He wore torn jeans, a gray T-shirt and a leather bomber jacket that looked as if it had been through a thresher. He was a sharp contrast to the polished perfection of Charme and its diners, a collection of people confident about where they belonged in New York City and life.

She felt a little pang of sympathy for him, even if she knew he'd brought this on himself. In her email to him, she'd noted that dress was business casual. And yet… Somehow she knew he would have felt even more out of place if he'd dressed the part. The clothes he was wearing were a shield. Against the restaurant, against what was being demanded of him, against what she was about to put him through.

Mark's rough baritone cut clear through the murmur

of cultured lunchtime conversation. "It's not like I'm trying to come in here without a shirt or shoes."

Diners were turning to look now, pausing in their midday negotiations and machinations to watch the entertainment.

The hostess responded quietly, probably asking Mark to leave, or warning him that she'd get the manager. She was just a kid, nineteen or twenty at most, and she looked panicky.

"Where does it say I can't wear whatever the hell I want?"

Haven could see the hostess's agitation. She pushed her seat back, moving slowly without drawing attention to herself. She wanted to cut this off before he got physical or threatening, before he got himself kicked out. She knew bar brawls were among his specialties, and though she'd never read about him hurting or even yelling at a woman, she didn't want this to be his test case.

Nearly tripping where the wide gray floor gave way to the carpeted entryway, she caught herself and stepped behind Mark with her dignity intact. "He's with me."

Mark and the hostess both turned to look at Haven. The hostess's eyes were hostile, Mark's dark and dangerous.

"We've met," Haven told the hostess. "I was here a week ago Friday, too. You seated me."

"Yes," said the hostess. "I remember you. Nevertheless, we ask that our patrons observe our—"

"I missed Ryan when I was here Friday. Is he in today? I'd love to say hi to him."

Ryan Freehey was Charme's owner, and everything

about the hostess's stance shifted from aggressive to submissive at the mention of his name. "He's not in today, but I'd be happy to tell him you were here and asking for him."

"Thank you. I appreciate that. Tell him Haven Hoyt says hi."

Haven turned to Mark. Why hadn't she insisted on meeting him in her office? Well, she'd have to make the best of it. She stuck out her hand. "Haven Hoyt."

His eyes narrowed.

She guessed if you were Mark Webster, dressed in beatup clothes and girded for battle, she might not be a sight for sore eyes, but she was pretty damn proud of today's outfit—high-waisted wrap skirt with skinny belt, cute cropped sweater, print blouse and beige espadrille-style shoes stacked so high she felt downright precarious. Her hair was piled up on her head, and she'd checked her makeup before she left the office. She looked good.

Plus she'd just saved his butt.

So why was he staring at her as though she was a bug on his dinner plate?

She dropped her hand, because he obviously wasn't going to shake it.

"Wait," said the hostess. "You're—" Her gaze journeyed over Mark, assessing him. Her sour expression summed up how far Mark had fallen from his prettier days, but the hostess gamely said, "I *love* 'Twice As Nice'!"

"You weren't even born when—"

Haven intervened swiftly. "It's a great song, isn't it?" she gushed. "A huge hit!"

She used his arm to swivel him away from the hostess stand and led the way to their table.

Haven was conscious, as she walked, of his eyes fixed on her back, boring into her. Her heart beat fast with nerves from the near confrontation.

She didn't bother to wait for him to pull out her chair for her—she knew *that* wasn't going to happen. She sat, and he dropped into his chair with a masculine nonchalance that made her breath catch. He shrugged the mangled bomber jacket off his shoulders and let it drop down the back of his chair. His fitted gray T-shirt revealed sculpted biceps and well-defined pecs. He'd apparently been working out, between bouts of hiding in dingy bars and getting himself photographed staggering drunk. She could do a lot with a body like that.

In the purely professional sense, that was.

She'd been at this restaurant Friday night with a very nice, painfully boring hedge-fund manager. All of her recent blind dates had been as stimulating as a trip to the grocery store. Haven had to admit that, as messy as Mark was making this lunch, it was a hell of a lot more interesting than any of those dates. He was a lot better looking, too. Gruff, badly dressed, in need of a shave, but he still had presence. Another point in his favor.

He pulled out his phone and studied it as if it was going to save him. From her?

From himself, she suspected. Because whatever had brought him to Charme today, he *really* didn't want to be here.

Might as well get it out on the table. "You're not meeting me of your own volition, right?"

"No." He had nice eyes, gray-blue under slashes of brow, a mobile mouth and amazing bones. She'd have to make sure he got some sleep and quit—or at least cut back on—the partying.

"You want to tell me why you came?"

"They have some look-alike they say they'll use instead of me for the tour if I don't clean up my act. And apparently you are the official act cleaner upper."

She smiled at that. "I am the official act cleaner upper."

"You've got your work cut out for you."

He wasn't the first client to have said that to her, but he was the first to have said it with such belligerence. Most were apologetic. On the other hand, most hadn't been photographed nude with five women at once or been kicked out of several newsworthy A-list parties.

"So you're thrilled to be here."

"Here in the specific sense of Charme—" he pronounced it "charm" with no hint of French "—or in the larger sense of in your hands?"

She wouldn't mind having him in her hands in the nonprofessional sense. *Yikes*, had she actually thought that? He was *so* not her type, great body or not. "I meant in my hands, but clearly you're not thrilled to be here, either."

"That depends entirely on who's picking up the tab."

Oh, she *did* have her work cut out for her.

Haven had debated whether or not to take Mark on, knowing he was going to be a royal pain. She'd consulted some of her colleagues, who'd also been split on the question. Some thought it would be the perfect opportunity for another high-profile coup to cement Haven's recent successes—her elevation of Amanda Gile and of party-girl Celine Carr. Others warned her that it was one thing to rehab the image of a rising star with some impulse issues and quite another to try to bring back a man who'd been a celebrity zombie for close to a decade.

What had finally convinced her to accept Mark as a client was the networking potential. She'd been trying to build a relationship with the band's manager for years. If she could make Mark look good, there'd be other opportunities in the future.

If she couldn't—well, there was no point in thinking about that. She hadn't gotten this far by doubting herself.

"Lunch is on me," she said mildly. It was like working with puppies. If you were calm and firm, and they didn't sense your agitation, you'd be fine.

The waiter who approached their table managed not to react to her client's garb. "Can I start you with a drink?"

"Do you have a beer list?"

The waiter rattled off the beers and Mark chose one. She ordered a glass of sparkling water with lemon.

"Do you need a few more minutes?"

"Yes—" she began, because Mark hadn't even picked up his menu, but he interrupted her.

"Any kind of steak will be fine."

"We have a very nice beef tender—"

"That's fine."

She ordered seafood pasta.

Mark's posture was as angry as the rest of him, head down, shoulders hunched, protecting himself from the world. They could start there—but not today. Today she'd just talk to him. Loosen him up a little, if that was even possible. "So, the tour's this fall?" It was March now—not a lot of time, but enough. She'd changed Amanda Gile's life in six months.

"Yeah." It was barely a word, just a notch above a grunt.

"Will there be an album?"

"We'll release cuts from the tour itself as singles for download. If there's enough good material, we'll make an album." He rolled his eyes to indicate what he thought the likelihood of that was.

"And everyone's on board?"

He averted his gaze. "Not Pete."

Pete Sovereign was the other guitar player. The one Mark had punched in the face ten years ago, leading to the band's breakup. There'd been something about a woman, a groupie, they'd both slept with. The groupie had had unkind things to say about Mark afterward to the press. Haven couldn't help being reminded of her own romantic past, even though the situations were different and hers hadn't been public. Maybe that was where the unexpected twinges of empathy for Mark had come from. She probably needed to shut that down. A few similarities didn't make them bosom buddies.

The two men hadn't spoken since the incident—or so Google had informed her.

She doubted she'd pry any more info about that out of him today. And it probably didn't matter much. She had her marching orders. Take one hostile, scruffy, washed-up musician and produce a creditable version of the pretty, dimple-faced boy he'd been.

At least Amanda Gile had cut and styled her hair regularly and worn fashionable clothes.

A thought occurred to her. "Who's getting Pete on board?"

For the first time, she saw an emotion cross his face that might not have been pure anger, though she wasn't sure what it was.

"Oh, God, they're making you do it," Haven guessed.

He nodded. "Those were the terms. Work with you and kiss Pete Sovereign's ass." Their eyes locked and she could see the emotion, for a split second, clearly.

Pain.

She didn't know exactly what had gone down between him and Pete all those years ago, but whatever it was, it hadn't been pretty.

She had her work cut out for her, but he did, too. Grovel to Pete Sovereign. Remake himself.

The compassion she'd felt when she'd first seen him in his raggedy clothes, haggling with the hostess, came back in a wave. Which was weird, because she rarely mourned people's "old selves," rarely had qualms about rehabbing their images. She believed in image. Image was its own armor, and donning it could make you ready for anything. Even so, people could be resistant. Sometimes they had ideas about wanting to be themselves or not wanting to be fake. In those cases, Haven reassured them that the right image wouldn't be like that. It would feel as though they were showing their best selves to the world. *Let me show you how to wear the real you on the outside.*

She didn't expect that argument to fly with Mark. He was too smart, too cynical. Too sure his best self was already showing.

"Can I ask you something? Given how much you obviously don't want to work with me or apologize to Pete Sovereign, why are you doing the tour? What are you hoping to get out of it?"

The look he gave her could have lasered through glass, sheared it off clean. "Do we have to analyze it? I'm here, right? What if I just tell you I need to do this?"

"That's fine," she said, and watched his shoulders sink with relief.

It would be helpful to know who he was, what he was about, but strictly speaking, no, she didn't have to know his motivations to do her job. She just had to get him cleaned up, *keep* him cleaned up and present him to the public eye at events where journalists would make a stink about his new, clean-cut self and the boozing, womanizing wreck he'd renounced.

She'd keep it simple, do her job and deliver a shiny new version of Mark Webster to his manager, as promised. Which meant she couldn't waste time on sympathy or curiosity or any other extraneous emotions. She was an artist, Mark Webster was her medium and she had work to do.

MARK'S STEAK WAS AWESOME, no two ways about it. It was worth the awkwardness of this whole stupid scene, worth eating in this sterile black-and-gray room with the other stiff-backed diners, worth getting waylaid by the teenaged hostess and her judgmental eyes, worth being head-shrunk by Haven Hoyt. Mark could almost slice the tenderloin with the side of his fork and the flavor was amazing. He loved it when meat tasted like meat, not frou-frou ingredients.

Concentrating on the food also made it easier to keep his gaze off Haven's breasts, which otherwise were… They were the eighth wonder of the world. He was surprised the other diners weren't magnetically drawn right out of their seats to stare. Every time he lifted his eyes from his steak, he had to focus like a madman on her face and not on her curves. He didn't know what she was wearing—the bottom part was like a burlap sack with a riding crop tied around the waist, and the top part was a 1970s-style button-down shirt under an absurdly short sweater—but whatever she'd engineered underneath her clothes should be part of the building plan for the next generation of bridges. He could practically feel her against his palms. His hands curved involuntarily.

It would probably be a bad idea to proposition her, but that was what he really wanted to do. He wanted to do that a hell of a lot more than he wanted to have a conversation with her about whitewashing his bad self.

She was asking him another question. "Do you have a look in mind you want to achieve? Besides 'pop star'?'"

Pop star had never been a look he aspired to. It had been a look he'd stumbled into, that he'd worn like too-tight clothing. And it sucked to think it was now something he had to work to attain. He shook his head.

"Particular people you want to see? Places you want to go?"

"I'm just not that guy."

She nodded, like that made sense to her. Well, that was something.

He already saw the people he wanted to see—the guys he played blues with in the crappy little club in the Village, and the ones he shot hoops with at the gym near his apartment in Queens. But he was pretty sure that wasn't the answer she was looking for. Haven Hoyt's people to see and places to go were in a whole different league than his.

"I'm going to set up a bunch of appointments for you—hair, nails, skin." She touched her hair and stroked the hot pink slickness of her own nails as she spoke, and his body heated. He had to look away. "For clothing, I'll bring in a personal shopper—we can keep it simple at a department store."

He hadn't shopped anywhere other than his local secondhand store in nearly a decade. The whole idea made his skin crawl. He still remembered the way it had felt to be fussed over and groomed like a baby monkey when he was in the band. He didn't miss that, not for a second.

He itched to get away from her scrutiny and her plans as intensely as he'd wanted to touch her earlier. His primitive brain screamed, *Run away.*

"Can't I just promise I'll get a haircut and buy some new clothes?"

A half smile appeared on Haven's glossy lips as she tugged a bite of pasta off her fork. She shook her head.

"I hate this."

He hadn't meant to say it out loud, but he *liked* Haven, and something about her loosened his lips. She wasn't a ballbuster, and she didn't come off fake. She had a way of looking at him that, yeah, maybe bordered on pity, but it was better than the other brands of female attention he usually got—scorn or leftover band worship from self-destructive women who wanted to flush their self-esteem down the toilet with him.

"I'll try to make it hurt as little as possible."

She said it without sexual emphasis, but it still made the blood rush out of his brain. He bet she would. If he swept the utensils and plates off the white cloth, the table would make the perfect surface on which she could make it hurt, or not, as she pleased. He'd take it either way.

Only he wouldn't. Because women like Haven Hoyt didn't sleep with men like him. He could tell by looking at her that, despite the softness of those curves, she had a thick, hard shell. He'd bounce right off if he tried to get through. But knowing that didn't stop him from craving Haven and her sleek black hair and riveting mouth. The steak had become tasteless and chewy, and he hastily redirected his thoughts. No point in missing the prize he could have to fantasize about the one he couldn't.

"I'll get you a schedule as soon as I can. It'll have the makeover stuff on it and then a whole bunch of events you and I will appear at."

He set his fork down at the side of the plate. "Events."

"Parties, concerts, clubs—we're going to take you out on the town so you can get photographed and written about. Otherwise, your new image isn't going to do you any good."

He tried not to let it show on his face how much he dreaded "events." How much he loathed the people and the publicity, the fakery, the exposure. "It's not going to do me any good."

She tilted her head to one side. "It could do you a hell of a lot of good. If you want to do this tour." Her eyes narrowed in scrutiny.

He couldn't turn away, and it probably wouldn't have helped, anyway. She'd see. He couldn't decide if he liked that, or if it terrified him.

"So—I'll ask you again. Why are you doing it?"

He still didn't want to answer the question, but he knew she'd keep asking him until he spilled. She was that kind of woman.

"I said no when they asked me, at first," he admitted.

Two of his former bandmates and his old manager had come looking for him after he hadn't returned their calls, showing up at Village Blues one evening to corner him.

You look like hell, man.

He'd run out of disposable razors a few days earlier, along with milk and cereal. That meant no shaving, and it also meant breakfast had been Bloody Marys in the neighborhood bar. Nothing new on either front.

Thanks, guys.

They'd bought him *several* drinks and then explained the situation. His bandmates needed money. They wanted to do a reunion tour. They were sure he needed money, too, how about it? Jimmy Jeffers, the manager, would make it happen.

He'd told them no. In much stronger language, a burst of fiery self-righteousness that had felt better than sex.

They'd backed off, right out of the club. He'd thought it had been the persuasive power of his refusal, but probably they'd already decided they could replace him. His assholery had only reinforced their intention to do so.

"You know the band's history?" he asked Haven.

She nodded. Her hair was up in some kind of fancy twist thing. He wondered how many hairpins it took to keep it there, how much hair spray. She was so flawlessly put together, the kind of woman he didn't waste his time pursuing. Different worlds, different values. But Haven wasn't looking through him. She was looking at him with sharp, knowing, *memorizing* regard.

"What that history *doesn't* say is that I never should have been in Sliding Up in the first place. I'm not popstar material, and anyone could have seen that by looking at me. I was going to school at Berklee, playing blues and rock and roots, and I let myself get snowed by a producer, which is what happens to a lot of musicians. Labels go after young guys in crappy circumstances who can't say no. I should have had the balls to refuse, because I had other options."

"So why did you eventually say yes to the reunion?"

"My dad had a stroke. A few weeks ago."

Her face softened. She'd been pretty before, but now looking at him as though she cared—

It pissed him off that he still had this weakness in him. He hadn't learned that women could do this at will—listen raptly, make you think you were the only man in the world. He hardened his heart and plowed on.

"He's got months of physical rehabilitation ahead of him and a nurse taking care of him in his house. The bills are a bitch and his crappy insurance barely makes a dent. I'm his only kid. My mom's dead. I told him I'd take care of it."

"That was kind. You're a good son."

He waved it off. "I'm not, really. He and I hadn't spoken for years. He raked me over the coals for being a screwup and—I lost my appetite for getting reamed out every time I had a conversation with him. But when this happened, I realized he's not going to be around forever. I want a chance to have a father-son relationship with him. And it's the right thing to do."

Her eyes softened a little more, and he tried not to like it.

"So you agreed to do the tour."

"Jimmy didn't tell you all this?"

She shook her head.

"Did he tell you they were holding a replacement over my head? Someone who looks like me, plays the guitar, can lip sync a hell of a lot better than I can and doesn't need you to dress him in the morning?"

She bit her lip, another partial smile. "I don't think you need me to dress you."

She stopped right there, perfectly innocent, but his dirty brain knew exactly what it wanted to say back.

Nah. I'd rather have you undress me.

The thought got a grip on his dick. *Nice work, schmo. Make this even worse on yourself.*

"So, they can replace you. That must be weird." She leaned across the table. *Keep your eyes on her face.* And it was no hardship. Her nose was long and elegant with a slight upturn at the very tip. Her eyes were greenish, her skin pale and creamy. He wanted to taste it. His tongue tingled.

He needed another beer as soon as humanly possible, but the waiter was nowhere in sight.

He'd lost the thread of their conversation. "What'd you say?"

"I said it must be weird to feel like you're replaceable."

Now she sounded like a shrink again.

The truth was, it pissed him off how easily they could drop another man into his slot. Which was stupid because he'd known that pop groups like Sliding Up were just pretty illusions that presented the music some producer dreamed up. And there was nothing—*nothing*—about the job that he wanted, except the money.

Or so he told himself. But if he didn't want the job, why was he so pissed? He hated to think he still had the same old craving for fame and fortune that had gotten him in trouble in the first place. The desire to have an arena full of people telling him with their applause and their screaming that his music was worth something… when he knew all too well it wasn't.

"Whatever," he said, because she was too much—too pretty, too sympathetic, too easy to talk to. Because he had this feeling that she wouldn't want to stop with messing with his hair, his clothes, his nightlife. She'd want to open him up and make him over from the inside out. And there was no way she was getting in there. "It's fine. I need the money, I'll do the tour, I'll live with their stipulations."

He would let the exquisite Haven Hoyt put her hands all over him (metaphorically) and turn him—but only the external him—into some version of himself he wouldn't recognize.

She was still looking at him as if she could see right through him. He wondered what the hell she saw.

Maybe the truth. How much it sucked that he needed the tour, sucked that the only way to help his dad was to sell himself out—again.

Or maybe she saw what he saw most of the time when he looked inside.

Failure.

2

"No more hedge-fund managers."

Haven leaned over Elisa Henderson's broad desk and smacked its surface for emphasis. She had to find a blank space between all the photos Elisa kept of the couples she'd match-made over the years. Brides in white, husbands and wives romping across tropical beaches on their honeymoons and even a few couples mooning over swaddled-up newborns and fat-cheeked infants. Haven had plenty of satisfied clients, but even she had to admit that you couldn't beat Elisa's job for visible results.

Her dating coach frowned at her. "You've already said no more lawyers, no more surgeons and no one who's involved in any way in film. You stipulated up front you wanted a successful, independent, professional man who dresses well. That right there makes the field pretty narrow. You can't keep eliminating whole categories of men. Next you'll be saying no chest hair."

The thought had crossed Haven's mind, but she kept

her mouth shut. She did like things smooth, metaphorically and literally.

She had a quick flash of Mark Webster's decidedly un-smooth face. Probably only because she'd spent so much time staring at it, trying to picture how it would look clean shaven. The last time he'd been photographed without stubble, he'd been considerably younger.

"Haven."

"Sorry, just thinking about work."

"Can we agree? No more eliminating whole categories of men?"

"No one in finance," Haven amended.

"That's even *worse*. That's half the professional, well-dressed men in the city."

"And no musicians," Haven said, thinking of Mark again. He was *not* going to be an easy project. He *hated* the idea of the tour. Money was forcing his hand, and that never made for a good situation.

"I'd already eliminated musicians. They don't tend to be well dressed, at least not according to your vision of what well dressed entails."

For Haven, that involved a suit, or at least pressed slacks and a dress shirt hanging on broad shoulders. An expensive leather belt around a narrow waist. It was possible she was salivating slightly at the thought. She'd been sex deprived too long for her own good.

Haven had hired Elisa after Elisa had pulled a surprise two-match victory out of a tricky dating–boot camp weekend. Both Haven and Elisa had briefly looked like fools as their shared client, Celine Carr, tromped all over a Caribbean island sucking face with a paparazzo, while her two handlers chased after her and failed to catch up. But just when it had seemed that nothing good could come out of the weekend, Elisa had realized that Celine and her paparazzo, Steve Flynn, were head over heels for each other, and she'd managed to make a splash of it on national television. On top of that, she'd found true love herself with a former friend-turned-lover on the trip.

Haven had been so impressed that she'd signed up for Elisa's Love Match package, which included both advice and actual matches. Elisa didn't always make matches. Sometimes she just poked and prodded from behind the scenes. But Haven felt as though she'd exhausted enough possibilities on the island of Manhattan that she'd better seek new blood. She wanted access to Elisa's top secret, intensely coveted, *expensive* database.

Elisa tucked her auburn hair behind her ears. "I think you might need to adjust your criteria."

"What's wrong with my criteria?"

"You say you want all these things—educated, polished, well dressed, well spoken, a good earner—but then you go out with the guys I pick and say they're leaving you cold. What if you opened up the field a little? Tried someone a little different?" Elisa tapped a few keys and brushed the trackpad, then turned the laptop around so Haven could see. "Check this guy out. Teaches rock climbing, former Navy." Elisa ticked off his claims to fame. "Does have a fondness for wool socks and hiking boots, so as you might imagine he's kinda outdoorsy—"

"Stop." Haven held up her hand and noticed that

she'd somehow chipped one Screaming Pink finger-
nail. She had the color in her drawer at work—she'd
patch it when she got back to the office. "Outdoorsy?
Seriously? Look. At. Me."

Elisa did as Haven asked, an appraisal as coldly
clinical as a doctor's exam. Not at all the way Mark's
gaze had felt yesterday. His scrutiny had melted over
her skin like warm butter. She thought of saying something about that, but she suspected Elisa would take
altogether too much glee in it. She might even cite it
as proof that Haven was barking up the wrong dating tree. But Haven wasn't. She knew what mattered,
and for better or for worse, image was a big part of it.
It was what she'd made her career on. It was who she
was. And she needed a guy who could appreciate its
importance.

"Like seeks like," Haven told Elisa.

She could picture him. At least six feet. Dark hair,
close-cropped but not so short she couldn't run her fingers through it. Dark eyes. Tailored clothes. Athletic.
Professional—maybe a CEO of a Fortune 500 company.
Or, she wasn't *that* picky—he could be a small business
owner, too. Just—successful. Refined. At ease with social events and people.

"Okay, I admit, you're not terribly outdoorsy. But
I don't think like always seeks like. Look at me and
Brett."

"But you are alike. Education, background, socio-
economics, level of polish."

Haven hadn't worried about any of that in her
last serious relationship. Poet Porter Weir had worn

consignment-shop artist's garb to go with his longish hair and his intense, *life is nasty, brutish and short* gaze.

Haven had met him at a poetry reading she'd attended when her mother and sisters were visiting New York.

Haven had somehow been born into the wrong household of brilliant, passionate, neo-hippy women. As a child, Haven had loved her family but never quite felt as though she fit in with their crafty projects and eco-adventures and thinky ideas. She was like a Limited Edition Fashion Barbie among handcrafted fabric dolls made by a fair-trade cooperative in Lima, Peru.

On this particular New York trip, she had done her best to make her family feel comfortable—taking them to out-of-the-way galleries, artists' studios and literary events. She'd felt like a fish out of water, much as she had as a child, when her mother had introduced her sisters and then added, with a wry twist to her mouth, "And this is my princess, Haven." Maybe in some families, "princess" would have been a compliment, but Haven had known from the time she was very little that in her case it wasn't. She was decidedly outside the freewheeling, new-age family her mother had dreamed of.

At the poetry reading, Porter Weir had walked past all her sisters in their fun, colorful peasant clothing, their soft, flowing hair and natural faces. He'd made straight for her, in her of-the-moment New York fashion and her pinned-up hair and perfect makeup. He asked her what she thought of his poetry, how it made her feel. And it had been such a long time since anyone had asked her how anything made her feel that she'd found herself answering.

He'd wanted *her*. And in the early days of the relationship he had made her feel not only beautiful, but also smart, interesting and creative. Still, she could never shake the fear that if he looked too closely, he'd discover that she was far more princess than poetess.

And that was more or less what had transpired. He'd dug deep and been deeply disappointed.

Haven had never told Elisa what had happened between her and Porter. She'd mentioned him, of course, because he was her most recent serious relationship. But she'd said only that they'd been too different.

"The point is," Haven concluded, "I don't do outdoorsy."

Elisa nodded, admitting defeat, then hit a button on her computer and made the former Navy guy disappear. "It was just a thought."

"Next." Haven had to get back to her own work soon, but Elisa's office always felt like a refuge. If Haven had had time for therapy, she would have wanted it to feel like this. Cozy and friendly and with a splash of humor.

Elisa laughed. "Okay. Try this." She displayed another man on the screen. "He's the vice-president of marketing for a well-known jewelry maker. Think expensive Christmas gifts."

Haven was already a beat ahead of Elisa, hoping for diamond studs. "Wardrobe?"

"He's wearing a rumpled jacket in this picture."

Haven leaned in. Dark hair, dark eyes. The jacket was indeed rumpled, but that was only one small strike against him. Maybe it had been raining the day the photo was taken.

"He likes to 'dine out,' 'socialize with friends,' and 'go to the movies.'"

"Why haven't you shown me this guy before?" Haven demanded.

"Honestly? Because this profile bores me to tears."

"Maybe he's just not that good at—"

Elisa scrunched up her face, and they both started laughing.

"Right," said Haven. "He's in marketing. He should be able to write a profile of himself that makes him sound worth meeting. But honestly? I'm in PR and I could never write those profiles. If I made them too cute, I always felt like I was fake, and if I made them honest, they sounded boring."

"That's why you have me to do it for you," Elisa said. "So it's up to you. Do you want to give this guy a chance?"

"He sounds perfect."

"Okay, let's go for it. I'll set something up for this weekend. And I'll gently suggest that he wear something a little more—pressed—than what he's got on in this photo."

"That sort of spoils it, if you have to tell him, right?"

"Well," said Elisa with a mischievous grin, "if it gets him laid, maybe he'll learn from it."

"Who said anything about anyone getting laid?"

Elisa looked up from the laptop screen. "How long, exactly, are you planning for your current dry spell to last?"

"Why break something two years in the making?" Haven winced.

"As someone who has recently broken a two-plus-year dry spell, I have to recommend it. The breaking, not the spell."

"Do you think it was the breaking that was so good? Or the man you broke it with?"

"Probably the man." Elisa smiled dreamily.

Haven wondered if being happily matched was a boon or a liability for a dating coach. On one hand, if Elisa could do so well for herself, it said something for her emotional intelligence. On the other, Haven suspected most single women would be more likely to confide in a dating coach who didn't seem quite so smugly settled.

Elisa snapped out of her reverie. "The point is, you don't *have* to find the perfect man to break the losing streak."

"Sex is a lot of work. If I'm going to do it, it'd better be good."

Elisa narrowed her eyes. "Sex is a lot of work? Are you doing it right?"

"Pumice stones and moisturizers and Brazilians and lingerie shopping and the good sheets and candles and—"

"It's not an Olympic event, Hav," Elisa interrupted. "You're allowed to just do it. Like on the living room couch, drunk, and with the full complement of God-given body hair."

Haven knew from personal experience that while guys might claim not to need things groomed and romantic and perfect, over time they would come to crave the fantasy version. Once the early, oblivious bliss wore off, Elisa would find that out, too.

"If it's worth doing, it's worth doing right," Haven said.

Elisa crossed her arms. "Are we talking about 'right'? Or are we talking about 'looking good'?'"

"When it comes to men, there's no difference."

Elisa gave her a hard look. "I'm a dating coach. There's a difference."

"I'm an image consultant. There's not."

Elisa laughed. "Agree to disagree." She shut the laptop and came around the desk as Haven stood. "You're a hoot, girl."

Elisa put her arm around Haven, and Haven rested her head on Elisa's shoulder, glad Elisa thought it was funny. But she hadn't been joking. When it came to men, image was everything.

MARK STEPPED INTO Mad Mo's and was assaulted by screens and vintage neon signs, piped music and raised voices. Even years of having his ears blown out on a stage and in blues clubs hadn't made him immune to the overstimulation. He had to pause in the doorway to get his bearings.

Mad Mo's had been around since the 1940s, and it was the antithesis of the place where he'd had lunch with Haven yesterday. At Charme, everything was calculated and calculating, from the color scheme to the people who chose to put themselves on display there. Here—well, it had all happened through year after year of accidents. Someone had once given Mo a neon beer sign and then he had become a known collector of them. The art on the walls was a mélange of photos of Mo's family, crayon pictures kids had drawn and postcards from every corner of the world. And the food was— It was just food, the fries spilling over the top of the burgers, pickle wedges stuffed wherever they'd fit. Haven Hoyt would have a heart attack if she saw this scene. She'd want to call up whichever of her friends was responsible for giving restaurants image makeovers and have them here before close of business.

Earlier that day Haven had sent him a color-coded spreadsheet that laid out his fate at a series of fund-raisers, openings, soirees and cocktail parties. Nothing in her schedule—not even the two-hour appointment at the high-end barber or the afternoon of shopping at the department store—had struck as much fear in his heart as the text Jimmy had sent him a couple of hours ago, telling Mark to meet him and Pete Sovereign at Mo's.

Mark had called Haven for help and together they'd worded an apology. She was sorry she couldn't accompany him to Mo's but she had to attend an event. She told him she had faith in him; he should just deliver the apology and get out, fast.

While he'd needed the help in getting the words right, he was grateful she wasn't with him. It would have felt too much like having a babysitter. Better to face up to Pete and do his best.

And so he was here. He kept putting one foot in front

of the other, trudging toward what felt like his doom. *Love you, Dad. Doing this for you.*

He lifted his gaze and found Jimmy in the crowd, beanpole tall and narrow faced. His former manager waved him toward the wide bar that formed a U on one side of the restaurant. Pete was leaning on the bar, his blond bangs hanging in his eyes, as insufferably cocky-looking as he'd been the last time Mark had seen him. Mark was a poor judge of male beauty, but he'd never gotten Pete's appeal to women. He looked—to Mark— like an overgrown kid. Countless promoters and image consultants had championed Pete's boyishness back in the day, claiming he was popular precisely because teenaged girls didn't really want men. They weren't ready for them yet. Body and facial hair still secretly scared them. They wanted the illusion of innocence. Hence the appeal of the barely-past-boyhood pop group.

Mark crossed to the bar and Jimmy clapped him on the shoulder, as if they were friends. "Hey."

"Hey."

Years ago, Mark had believed that Jimmy liked him. Jimmy was a straight shooter, and Mark had been, too. In an industry that was full of hot air, that was a rare commodity. This last week, though, had made it clear how little Jimmy thought of the man Mark had become—and how unnecessary he considered him to the tour.

It would be humbling, if there were anything in him left to be humbled.

Behind Jimmy, Pete shifted but didn't step forward to

greet him. He wasn't going to make it easy for Mark. And as much as Mark hated him, he couldn't blame him.

Moment of truth. He had to lower himself enough to apologize to the piece of dung leaning on the shiny teak bar. Otherwise, all the image rehabbing in the world wasn't going to make this tour happen.

Pete's arrogant half smile made Mark think of Lyn. Her beauty, her passion and her promises, the romantic ones and the professional ones. Pete had taken away not just those promises, but something deeper, something Mark had never been able to get back.

The noise in Mad Mo's formed a cushion around Mark, making everything feel faintly unreal. It still seemed possible to turn and leave, without consequences. His father and the medical bills were far away.

Jimmy shifted uncomfortably. Pete's smile grew bigger and more smug, the smile of a man who knew his opponent was between a rock and a hard place. Mark wondered how much of this Pete had orchestrated. Did he even give a shit whether or not Mark apologized? Did he just want to see Mark squirm? Had sending Mark to Haven been Pete's idea? He could imagine Pete howling with laughter at the notion of Mark undergoing an image rehab.

Jimmy gestured loosely toward Pete. "So, um—"

Mark's mouth refused to open. It was wrong, just dead wrong, that he should be the one apologizing.

Pete Sovereign boosted himself off the bar, giving Mark the full force of his superior grin and thrusting his hand out. "Nice of you to come all this way to beg."

For a moment, Mark could feel the world stretch and

shift—déjà vu. He could feel the moments that had just passed and the moments that were creeping up on them. He remembered how Pete's nose had given way to his knuckles ten years ago, and he imagined—no *lived*—with unapologetic clarity, the way Pete's cheekbone would crack under the force of the even more heartfelt blow Mark was about to deliver.

What stopped him from throwing the punch, oddly enough, was not thinking of his father. It was thinking of Haven Hoyt and the way she'd looked at him in Charme, her eyebrows slightly drawn together as if she were trying to figure him out. As if he were *worth* figuring out. And even when he'd called her about this meeting, Haven had not said anything about watching his temper or not getting in a fight. She had, in fact, told him he would be capable of handling it maturely.

He heard himself sigh, and he saw Pete's eyes widen. He leaned as close to Pete Sovereign as he could bear to, steeling himself against the guy's cologne, and said, "It will be a long, cold wait in hell for you if you think that's going to happen, douche bag."

Then he turned and walked out of Mad Mo's, the din fading behind him as the door swung shut and the cacophony of Manhattan's streets filled his ears.

3

"WHAT THE *HELL* were you thinking?"

There was something so incongruous about seeing Haven Hoyt in Queens, standing in the foyer of his apartment building, that it took him a moment to realize she was yelling at him. The hangover wasn't helping.

"Are you the most self-destructive human being on Earth?"

He almost answered her before he registered that her questions were rhetorical. "Did you come all the way out here to ask me that? Couldn't you have called?"

It was Saturday morning. Last night, Mark had walked as fast as his legs could carry him away from Mad Mo's and drowned his sorrows in shots of tequila at Over the Border. Countless shots of tequila. He'd gotten kicked out for harassing the bartender when she refused to serve him one more.

Haven crossed her arms. "I thought this bore discussing in person. Plus, I was so irritated with you that I needed to haul myself out here to burn off steam. Why do you live in Queens?"

"Because there's not enough room on the island of Manhattan for me and all my self-destructiveness."

A smile flirted with Haven's impeccably made-up face and vanished just as quickly. "Seriously, Mark, are you off your rocker?"

"Nope. I am totally sane. Pete Sovereign is, in fact, the biggest douche bag on Earth."

"Douchier than you? Because you're looking pretty douchey right about now. Throwing away a reunion tour and hundreds of thousands, possibly millions, of dollars. Screwing yourself and me out of a job."

Righteous fury made her even more beautiful. She kept tossing that glossy black hair, which she was wearing down today. It was perfectly straight and it looked like satin. Haven Hoyt was possibly made of satin from head to toe. Right now, he wanted to rub his entire greedy self all over her.

He caught himself mindlessly staring and attempted to corral some brain cells. "I take it you heard from Jimmy." Of course. Jimmy would have been on the phone to dismiss Haven almost before Mark's back had disappeared through the door. They'd have been glad to wash their hands of him, glad to have their low opinion of him confirmed.

"Jimmy called me this morning to, effectively, fire me," she said.

He hadn't wanted Haven to share the low opinion of him, though. That brought a mild sense of regret into his pounding head and foggy brain.

She teetered in strappy shoes with impossibly high, skinny heels. Not the right shoes for storming out to Queens in a temper. It was a good trek to his Sunnyside studio from the 7 line. This woman had impressive ankle strength and toe endurance.

Jesus, there was *nothing* sexy about either of those things. This was the twenty-first century, and naked feet were no longer the frontier. And yet, weirdly, he was turned on. Probably he would find her elbow sexy, or her toenail clippings, or—

He cast the closest thing he had to prayer skyward. If there were a remote possibility that he'd ever get to sleep with her, he wanted her to wear those shoes in bed.

"Haven, honestly? You should be glad to wash your hands of me."

She glared at him. "Can you let me be the judge of what I should be glad about? I wanted this job. I've been trying to show Jimmy what I can do for years. I need referrals from him."

"Well, then, I'm sorry. But I can't work with Pete Sovereign."

Even before the words were all the way out of his mouth, in the sober, hungover, head-splittingly bright light of day, he remembered that he had very few choices. And he didn't like the pitying way Haven was looking at him, head tilted to one side. As if he was too pathetic to be believed.

"What happened between you and that guy?"

There was no way he was going to tell her. He crossed his arms and leaned against the wall.

She sighed. "Fine. Don't tell me. I'll just take your

word that it was a big enough deal that you can let your dad rot because you're too proud to issue some meaningless apology."

He closed his eyes.

He could hear her breathing. Fast. Maybe the walk from the 40th Street station, maybe anger. With his eyes closed, he could imagine that was what her breathing would sound like if he got her worked up. If he licked around the rim of her ear, along the line of her neck, and down the curve of a breast.

Now he was breathing fast.

"You're going to have to find a way to work with Pete Sovereign."

His eyes flew open. Apparently, she was steel under all that satin. He could see it in her shoulders, in the hardness of her eyes. "It's none of your business."

"Too bad. I want this gig, and you're the gig. I begged Jimmy to give you one more chance. I begged on your behalf. You owe me this." Her eyes were challenging, her hands on her hips now.

"No. No way. I didn't ask you for anything and I don't owe you anything. I don't even know you." *Even if I have undressed you in my mind several times since the first time I laid eyes on you.*

"This isn't negotiable."

"There's no negotiation, Haven."

"There's me, standing here and telling you, you have to do this. Also, there's your dad. You said he needs a lot of physical therapy."

"Tons," Mark admitted. "Every day."

"And the nurse." She said it matter-of-factly, with the same sympathy that always undid him.

He couldn't speak. He just nodded.

"Mark. It doesn't have to be the world's most heartfelt apology. It just has to be *an* apology. This time I'll be there when you deliver it."

She'd moved from steel to supplication, and he could already tell it would destroy his resolve—that, and the implacable reality of his father's debt. Mark was crumbling inside, and there were no inner reserves with which to shore himself up. Haven's compassion had started his undoing, somehow, on Thursday. It was always the urge to let down your guard that killed you in the end.

"I don't want you there when I deliver it." As good as surrender.

"Well, tough luck," she said. "After last night's fiasco, I promised Jimmy I'd stick close to you for anything that might attract public attention until the tour."

Stick. Close. To. You. His pulse kicked up. "You agreed to follow me around for six months?"

"If that's what it takes."

"You really want this gig. You begged Jimmy Jeffers. You came all the way out here and—" He wasn't sure what to call what she'd done to him. Bossed. Pleaded. Unleashed something he wished she'd left pent up.

She didn't quite meet his eyes. "Yes." She scuffed the toe of her shoe lightly along the floor, and his eye followed the line of her leg. Today's skirt was more standard issue, black and midthigh length. Nice, lean, strong thighs he'd like wrapped around his waist.

"I like a good challenge, and you want to do this because you love your dad. And maybe because you've done nothing for the last ten years but play wedding gigs and make cameo appearances for screaming groupies. I can't imagine you find that very satisfying."

You forgot something, he wanted to say, with the same fervor that urged him to put his hands in her hair. *I want to do it because you're going to follow me around for the next six months. And even though I shouldn't want that, even though it's suicidally stupid for me to want that, even though you will never* mean *those looks you give me, I do. I want that.*

"No," he said instead, because she was right. "It's not very satisfying."

"So let me help you apologize to Pete Sovereign, okay?"

He understood defeat well. It was his friend. "Okay."

"And let me help you clean up your act, okay?"

"Okay."

She eyed him suspiciously. Smart woman. His motives were about as impure as it was possible for them to be. They were dirty and male and all about the dark secrets her body was keeping from him, the ones he wanted to unfurl, one sweet mystery at a time.

"Why are you suddenly so agreeable?"

You.

"Free haircut," he said, and she laughed, a real, open, musical laugh, and his heart pounded almost out of his chest.

HUNKS OF MARK WEBSTER's hair were hitting the floor, and Haven wasn't feeling as satisfied by that as she'd expected to.

They were in Caruso's, a high-end barbershop where Haven liked to take straight male clients. The chairs were covered in black leather, the rest of the furniture espresso and ebony. The sage-green walls displayed vintage photos of female movie stars, classy and sexy at the same time. These were the women Haven had modeled herself after when she'd realized that, as much as she admired them, she didn't want to be like her mother or her sisters.

Actually, she hated the way Mark's hair looked on the wide-plank wood floor, the softness of the pieces curled around nothing. The shorn look he had now revealed a pretty-boy quality he'd been hiding from the world for a long time. She wanted it to go back into hiding, because clean-cut Mark was doing something to her insides she didn't like at all.

The barber, Derek, had shaved Mark first. She'd watched the straight razor scrape over his skin. The blade moved like a caress, highlighting the strength of his jaw, his high cheekbones. Crazy-deep dimples flashed now when he smiled at her in the mirror, just often enough to keep her attention. She was standing there waiting for him to smile at her again. That couldn't be good, right?

"My hair hasn't been this short in, like, a decade. I didn't cut it for almost two years after the breakup."

Now the look he shot her in the mirror was more the usual Mark. Hard jaw, angry eyes. A little easier to take. She caught her breath, which made her realize she'd lost it, somewhere along the line.

"What made you cut it after two years?"

Just a flick of the smile, one corner. "I decided it was probably time to get laid again."

His eyes held hers. Too long. She looked away. She was uncomfortably hot in the pale blue suit jacket, but if she took it off, he'd see the sweat stains under her arms.

Her panties were damp, too, and she couldn't blame that on overdressing for the superheated barbershop.

"Did it work?"

Wait, why had she said that? She was flirting with him, prolonging the conversation. But she shouldn't. He was her client. He was—

Mark Webster, C.D. Certified Disaster.

He laughed, a rough, lovely sound, like something rusty from disuse. "Yup. The haircut worked the way it was supposed to. All the parts worked, too."

She didn't want to ask any more questions. Talking to Mark Webster about sex, with his eyes so big, long-lashed and luminous, his teeth so starkly white, was a bad idea. Removing all that hair should have made him more vulnerable, but she was the one rocked back on her heels.

She cast about for another topic. "I made an appointment for Pete to come see me next Tuesday morning in my office at ten."

He looked down at his lap, and she was sorry she'd gone there. Bad enough she was making him grovel without making him think about it today.

"It's not going to be so bad," she said. "Wham, bam—"

Whoops, that sounded like sex again, and the one-sided quirk of his mouth told her he hadn't missed that.

"I'll do most of the talking. You just deliver the line."

"I regret any lasting damage my temper has caused you," Mark intoned.

She was proud of the non-apology she'd crafted for him.

He frowned. "I don't think he's going to let me get away with it."

"Trust me."

Their eyes met in the mirror again, and he gave a short, hard laugh. "If I didn't trust you, do you think I'd let this guy put a straight razor on my throat? And cut my hair off? I feel like—Samson, right? Don't you sap my strength or something?"

He didn't look sapped. He looked...potent. She had to turn away from the mirror because his gaze kept catching hers and not letting go properly.

Mark Webster had a reputation in the media for saying and doing the wrong things, but he seemed to know the right way to get under Haven's skin. She was having a difficult time remembering why she shouldn't exchange smiles, meaningful glances and double entendres with him.

Right. *Right.*

Mark Webster was her client, and her job was *not* to land them both in the press as a seedy example of how to become his next castoff. He was a serial womanizer. By definition, that meant he was not interested in anything serious with her. And her job was to clean him up, not let herself be dragged into the mud.

"What do you think?" Derek asked her, warming some kind of expensive styling product between his

palms and smoothing it through Mark's hair, which
was now short enough to be "not long," but still had a
lot of wave. He had really great hair, thick and coppery
brown with streaks of lighter and darker colors. Women
paid fortunes for hair like that.

She was not secretly envying Derek for being allowed to run his fingers through Mark's hair. Not at all.

Oh, she was such a liar.

"It looks great," she said.

That, at least, was the truth.

"What do you think of the new, improved Mark Webster?"

It didn't matter how she answered, because she
couldn't *not* meet the ferocity of his unblinking challenge in the mirror. So he knew. He knew he looked
good, and he knew he was having an effect on her.

Derek very politely did not roll his eyes at them.

She wrenched her gaze away, but she couldn't stop
herself from putting her fingers to her wrist to feel the
way her pulse raced under the hot skin there, and when
she looked up again, Mark's eyes were on her.

JUDY, HAVEN'S FAVORITE personal shopper, kept touching Mark.

She brushed her fingertips briskly over his collar-
bone, tapped them thoughtfully on his muscled shoulders. "Hmm. Too tight through here. You're nice and
broad."

He *was* nice and broad. Haven's fingers tingled sym-
pathetically as Judy's moved. Haven wanted to check
out exactly where that seam fell on those excellent

shoulders, but she sat on her hands instead, lest they start dancing through the air with vicarious excitement.

They were in the large fitting area in the personal shoppers' suite, and Mark stood on a carpeted platform facing a three-way mirror. Today had included altogether too many mirrors, and she wished she didn't have to see Mark's reflection or her own flushed face anymore. He kept looking above the button of the suit jacket that restrained her breasts and meeting her glances with his intense gray-blue stare.

Her own clothes felt limp with heat and damp. Strands of her hair had come loose from her updo and now clung to her forehead and cheeks.

Haven Hoyt was not feeling very put together at the moment.

Judy tugged on the shirt to check the fit over Mark's pecs, brushing the cotton-silk blend across his chest as if there were a speck of dust she needed to remove. "Tough to fit you for a shirt when you're so big through here. That's a good thing." Judy looked up at Mark through her eyelashes.

Haven had never really thought about it before today, but Judy was attractive, for an older woman. She had platinum-blond hair and strong bones, and she looked great in her silver tunic, indigo jeggings and knee-high black boots. She seemed to be having fun.

Of course she was having fun, because she had her hands on Mark's chest. Haven had noticed his size the other day at lunch, but there was something about this particular blue dress shirt that emphasized his strength and bulk. Maybe it was just Haven's fond feelings for dress shirts, but more likely it was Mark. Judy kept messing with the buttons, as if making adjustments, but Haven was pretty sure her motives were baser.

Still, if Mark needed his buttons checked, Haven would be willing to help out. In fact, she might be willing to go to the mud pit with Judy for the privilege. And Haven didn't do muddy, any more than she did outdoorsy or sleep-in-a-big-T-shirt or *just have a few people over and I'm sorry I didn't have time to clean the house*.

Judy shamelessly ran her hand over Mark's butt— was that *really* necessary?—to emphasize the clean fit of the charcoal-gray dress pants. That butt was a mighty fine specimen, Haven mused, giving up on not having an opinion. It was firm and high and tight and round and she bet he knew how to use it to great advantage as leverage for—

"Nice line in front, too." All three of them stared at Mark's crotch in the mirror. Whatever Mark was packing under there was evident even under the "nice line" of expensive dress slacks. She briefly wondered whether it was arousing to have them both staring at his endowment like that. It would be pretty embarrassing to get an erection right now. Wouldn't it?

She raised her gaze from the front of his pants and found herself staring into Mark's eyes. He raised an eyebrow at her, and she watched her own face turn the same flaming pink as her nail polish. Heat swept through her, tightening her nipples and pooling between her legs. Mark's dimples deepened, even though his mouth didn't quite break into a full smile.

She wasn't going to make it. She was going to die of frustrated desire before the shopping session was over.

As much as she wanted to deny it, her body had decided this was foreplay.

She'd never been attracted to a client before. Never. She'd done image makeovers on male clients, and she'd sat in Judy's upholstered seat while Judy ran her hands over different sets of equally impressive shoulders, pecs and abs. Mark Webster should not have been any different, should not have been turning Haven's excellent brain to mush.

"I'm going to get some water," she said, and for that, she got a full-on Mark grin. It was a startling, marvelous thing, bright and white and all the way into his eyes, and she ran the hell out of that dressing area.

For the rest of the fitting, she stood at the far edge of the room, out of his sight in the mirror. He went through plain white T-shirts, a new, unscuffed leather bomber and several blazers and jackets. He tried on baseball jerseys and printed T's, fine-gauge sweaters and casual button-down shirts, ties, a pair of suspenders, new gym clothes.

He looked good in all of them. He looked as though they'd been made for him, as though he'd been sculpted to fill them perfectly.

Haven was fatigued from the effort of watching as Judy checked the fit of a raglan sleeve over Mark's substantial biceps, knelt at his feet to make sure the trousers broke over expensive Italian leather shoes the way she wanted them to and—this was the final insult—ruffled his hair as she placed a fedora in a ridiculously sexy tilt over one gray-blue eye.

Haven's only hope was that Saturday night with Jewelry Marketing Guy would turn out better than the last six or eight dates. Maybe Jewelry Marketing Guy would be so smart, so thoughtful, so interesting, so brimming with pheromones that she would want to sleep with him on the first date. Then she wouldn't need to imagine stripping Mark out of his formfitting new wardrobe, thrusting her fingers into his thick, scrumptious hair and pressing her mouth—actually, her whole freaking naked body—against his.

"Do I have to wear this stuff all the time?" Mark turned to ask her the question. Sullenly.

It was probably a good thing that he was still a pain in the ass. A hot, trouble-making, pain in the ass.

"Not when you're locked in your own apartment."

He sighed. "I hate you."

His eyes told her he didn't.

"I'll wear this home," he told Judy. He was in a gorgeous fine-knit striped V-neck sweater and butt-snugging jeans. Haven wanted to beg him not to wear those clothes out of the store. To have mercy.

He went to the men's room while Haven paid for his things. She'd bill the whole lot back to Jimmy, and Jimmy would take it out of Mark's tour earnings. God forbid Mark screw up again, because Haven had no idea who'd foot the bill if he torpedoed his chance to be part of the tour.

Judy handed Haven Mark's shopping bags, plus an unmarked plastic bag. "The clothes he wore in here,"

Judy said. "Unless you want me to just throw them in the trash right now. Or burn them."

Haven took the bags. She felt a peculiar tenderness for the ratty jeans and the tortured jacket, and on top of that she had a totally perverted desire to pull out the T-shirt and see if she could detect Mark's scent in it. Not the expensive hair-care products and fabric sizing from today, but the real Mark smell of coconut, leather and clean male sweat.

"Nah," she told Judy. "I'll give it to Goodwill."

"They might not want it. That jacket—"

"I know," Haven said fervently.

While she waited for Mark, she tucked the plastic bag of his clothes into one of the shopping bags, where it couldn't tempt her.

4

HAVEN DIDN'T HAVE a thing for celebrities. She liked to think that was a good trait in an image consultant, because she didn't freeze up or go all fangirl around them. She didn't fetishize fame or worship actors or read about British royalty with stars in her eyes. They were people just like anyone else, who had to do their jobs plus manage all of that expectation and public scrutiny.

Just people.

And, Haven would also have said about herself, Haven had *believed* about herself, that she didn't have a thing for musicians. As a teenager, she'd never screamed or launched herself onto a stage or pulled off her top because some hot musician had thrust his pelvis in her direction.

However, she was reconsidering her position, watching Mark Webster play the guitar at Village Blues.

She'd tried to get Elisa to come out with her, but Elisa had muttered something smug about a night in with her boyfriend who'd been on the road too much. So here

Haven was, sitting by herself at a little table in a dark club that was lit by a meandering string of white Christmas lights. She was sipping a glass of decent red wine and trying hard not to make eye contact with the motley assortment of men who made pre-makeover Mark look like a fashion plate.

Now she was glad she was here by herself, because she wanted to be able to ogle him without a perceptive female friend catching her at it. She didn't want to share the experience with anyone else, or process it out loud— she just wanted to watch him do what he was doing.

There was, of course, something inherently sexy about the guitar, about all that strumming and stroking, about the grip he had around its neck, sliding up and down while his other fingers worked in well-coordinated harmony. You couldn't *help* thinking about other things. Especially when the guitarist in question was Mark, with the jaw and the cheekbones, with the biceps that bunched and forearms that corded as his fingers clutched string to wood. He wore a form-hugging old T-shirt and ripped-up jeans—they'd bought them pre-ripped during the shopping spree, a compromise between his desire for well-worn and comfy, and her need for him to look like he hadn't dug his clothes from a Dumpster.

So, yeah, she was thinking about other things, but that was before he'd begun his solo.

She didn't know the tune, and she didn't know much about blues, but she knew passion. And the look on Mark's face, the rush of synchronized motion that came from his big, beautiful hands, the way his whole body contracted and arched, rocked and swayed—that was passion. He could coax the guitar to make sounds she didn't even know how to describe, crisp dots, sharp clenches, long wails of music. She bet he could make it say anything he wanted it to. She bet he could make it deliver a whole Shakespearean monologue.

Her mom and her sisters would love this guy, and she was sure he'd love them. Mark was a guy who lived big, lived out loud. Her mom gave whole workshops on this kind of thing—the authentic life, the artist's life.

She tried not to think about the look on his face and failed. There was no way she couldn't see it as a sex look. Her body was definitely reading it that way. It said he was following his bliss and following it all the way down.

It made her *feel* things.

For one, it made her wish she had something like that in her life, some creative outlet that could take her out of time, out of her body, and let her express herself the way Mark could. Her mom made pottery, and even though the bowls were misshapen and the sets never matched, her mom looked as if she was in heaven when she was up to her elbows in gray mud. Haven even owned a set. She just didn't...use them when people came over.

Sometimes she convinced herself that the apple hadn't fallen *so* far from the tree. Okay, she didn't create poetry or shape pots or make music. But she created celebrities and shaped images and made people.

Haven loved her job, and that was what mattered. And there were plenty of men out there who would respect what she did, love her ability to contribute financially, and enjoy being part of her social scene. She just needed to find one.

Under the spotlights, Mark took another solo, and now he was grinning at the guy across the stage from him and trading licks, each of them feeding off the other. It made her realize something about Mark she hadn't understood before. Why he resented the tour so much. Why he didn't want to be a pop musician, even if it would make money and let him help his father. Even if it seemed like the sort of thing no one in his right mind would turn down.

This was Mark, pouring himself into his music, his inner self on display for the whole room, in people's ears, throbbing in their skin, pulsing in their blood. Of course he didn't want to package himself up like some eighteen-year-old boy and make forgettable music for money.

The exchange between the two guitarists rose in intensity, toward frenzy. Like—

Like sex, she thought, of course. Mysteriously, miraculously, Mark Webster had the power to make Haven think about sex *all the time.* For two years, she'd hadn't felt much interest at all, and now...

Mark was in *her* ears, in *her* skin, pulsing in *her* blood. His music was making her wish for things she couldn't have. Making her wish Mark Webster would put his hands all over her. Grip and slide and stroke and strum.

PLAYING BLUES WAS Mark's therapy, and it felt good to be up on stage in that dark room, the noise so loud it rang like silence in his head as the music poured out of his guitar. His mind, his fingers and the strings were one. He loved being surrounded by a few of his favorite musicians and some ringers from the sign-up sheet, slipping into the groove, egging the other guitarist on, echoing a great riff from his buddy Jack on the Hammond B-3 organ. The drummer, someone he'd never seen before, wasn't half bad, a hot-shot conservatory kid. People were into it, too, tapping and chair dancing and dropping conversations to pay attention.

This was what he needed to drown out the confusion in his brain.

As he played, he pictured Haven Hoyt watching him in the mirror and his mind wouldn't let go of the image. Her eyes had wandered over him, a shameless scrutinizing and undressing he wouldn't have expected from a woman like her. She'd dropped her gaze when he met her eyes in the reflection, then peeked back as if to make sure he was still looking. A flirtation, even if she didn't know it or really mean it. It had boiled his blood, fast, and several times he'd had to force himself to think about Pete Sovereign in order to keep from sporting visible wood.

A hard game of basketball with the guys earlier in the evening, plenty of pushing and fouls, yelling, laughing, hadn't washed away the visual. None of it had brought his horniness back down to manageable. He couldn't stop thinking about her, wondering what she was like in bed.

The first time he'd met her, he'd thought her Teflon coating was too thick to penetrate, but he was far less sure now. He'd seen that blush sweep all the way down to her neckline. He bet if he got Haven's clothes off, got her under him, she'd be a spitfire. He bet she'd writhe and squirm and beg and whimper his name.

Oh, *hell*.

The front man, Devon, called "Seven Nights to Rock," a twelve-bar jump blues in A with a quick four, always a crowd-pleaser. People got up to dance, and through the path they'd cleared, he saw her. For a split second he thought he'd conjured her, voodoo'd Haven Hoyt right out of the dirtiest part of his mind. How else to explain what she was wearing? Some kind of top that tied around the waist and plunged deep between her breasts—was it possible she wasn't wearing a bra at all? The thought made him flub a riff he'd been working up. Because those breasts, sans support—

It was remarkably hard to imagine your hands on a woman's breasts and play the guitar at the same time, like two pathways in the brain colliding. His lust tripped over the notes and made a jangled mess of his music.

What the hell was she doing here? Coincidence? Or had she come down to hear him?

If she had, he told himself, it was out of professional interest. She had to know who she was dealing with on every axis if she were going to remake him, right? She had to know where he spent his time and whether he was dressed like she'd told him to.

He wasn't. He hadn't been able to bring himself to put on all those pretty-boy clothes. She'd kept his favorite jeans and bomber jacket. He'd meant to get them back from her, because there was no effing way he was going to let her dispose of them. He and that jacket had been to hell and back.

Sure enough, she caught his eye, pointed at his clothes—an old T-shirt and the jeans they'd picked out together today—and shook her head. But he thought she might be smiling. Just a little.

They finished up "Seven Nights" and started in on Delbert's "Squeeze Me In," and he couldn't help himself, he gave her a look. *Can you?*

Her gaze fled his, sought refuge anywhere it could get to. Then, as though she couldn't completely govern herself, she turned to him again. She met his eyes, and then her gaze dropped. Haven Hoyt was looking at his mouth. Jesus. Her expression was telling him, *Maybe so.*

No. He had to be making that up. No way this buffed-to-a-sheen, image-obsessed woman wanted him. He had proven that he could fluster her, but *wanting* was another thing entirely.

And what the hell difference would it make if she did? There was no way he wanted to get himself tangled up with her.

At the break between sets, she came over to him.

"You're amazing," she said. She had to lean close in the chaos, and her breath brushed his ear and sent signals he did his best to ignore.

He liked this way too much, her breath on his ear and her praise. He wanted to turn away so she wouldn't have a chance of seeing how much it meant to him. "Thanks," he said instead.

"You're crazy talented." Her face was so close to his that his hair prickled on his scalp.

He had to take a step back to keep himself sane. "Nah." She was wrong about that. He'd never had a deep enough well of musical talent, only been in the right place at the right time. "I just, you know, mess around."

"Do you play here a lot?" She was shouting.

He guided her, hand on her elbow, to a quieter corner of the room, where conversation, if not easy, was at least possible. "Whenever I can. And a few clubs in Queens and Brooklyn, too. There aren't many blues jams left anymore."

"I get it now," she said. "Why you hate the pop stuff. This is you, right? This comes from your soul."

He was startled by her words and by the rush of emotion and recognition he felt. He could only nod, and that felt inadequate.

"You ever tour?"

He laughed.

"Not with Sliding Up. Like, with these guys?"

She was wearing skinny jeans and knee-high boots, and he wanted to peel her like a banana. He had to force himself to stay in the conversation. "I don't have my own band. I play jams. Just for fun."

"But why not? Why not a band? You're good enough, Mark."

He shook his head. "I'm not. Just a dabbler. Besides, there's no money in blues. You have to play five nights a week, and even then, you have to have a day job."

"You used to teach music lessons, didn't you?"

"Where'd you hear that?" It was just one of the unnerving aspects of this thing with her, that she knew so much about him and he knew so little about her.

"I sniffed around," she said. "Talked to some of your old students, actually. They all said you dumped them."

"I didn't *dump* them." He heard the defensive edge in his voice and tried to tone it down. "I decided to stop giving lessons."

"You didn't like teaching?"

He shrugged. He didn't want to get into the whole reason he'd quit with the lessons.

"So—what do you do these days?"

"Like you said the other day. Live off Sliding Up's hit, do birthday parties for groupies and fans, play weddings and bat mitzvahs."

She made a face at him that suggested she knew how he felt about that. "Doesn't seem like you."

He shrugged. "What do you know about me?"

She turned away. She was blushing again, for a different reason this time, but his body chimed in anyway. His balls tightened, blood rushing into his cock. He liked her off balance. What did that say about him? He wasn't a nice man.

She fidgeted with the tie on her shirt, a gesture so un-Haven-like he wanted to reach out and still her hand. "I just—do they let you wear those ratty T-shirts when you play weddings?"

"I have a suit," he said. "Once in a while, I rent a tux."

"You told the hostess—" Her eyes narrowed.

"I was making a point."

"I should have guessed." She frowned. "I can't see you at a wedding, or with some little kid who's trying to figure out basic chords."

"I hate the weddings," he admitted. "But I loved the music lessons. Seventy percent of the time it was just paying the bills, but I'd get through to my students sometimes, or I'd see some talent in them, or a kid who was kind of dead, you know, would come alive playing. A parent tells you their kid won't do their homework, is flunking out of class, but practices two hours a day. It's a rush, then."

He was pretty sure he hadn't talked this much in years. He wasn't sure what had made him confess these things to Haven. She got him so heated up, and at the same time, lowered his defenses. It didn't make sense.

"Why'd you quit?"

She was looking at him as though she could see straight through him again. He was pretty sure she knew the answer to her own question, or at least had her theories. "I screwed up," he said. "Bunch of bad stuff happened in a row last year."

"The video?"

Yeah, she knew all right. He'd been caught on someone's iPhone, making out with two different women at the same party. Problem was, it wasn't the same party. There'd been no way to prove the two spliced-together clips were from different nights because he'd looked identical in them—same hair, same two-days' beard growth, same torn green T-shirt. He'd had his hands up one woman's shirt, down the other's pants. The thing went viral. "And then the DUI, a few days later. Meltdown city. Articles everywhere, blasting me for being a bad role model. You'd think the press wouldn't care anymore, they've always had this love-hate thing with me. And all those articles were right. I was a shitty role model. So I quit the music lessons. I had to stop pretending to be good for kids."

He'd toned down the drinking and the partying after that, too, and quit driving under the influence, but no one had reported on that.

"Your students—every single one of them—said you were the best teacher they ever had."

"They were just being nice."

"I don't think so." She tilted her head. "I want you to start again."

"What?"

"The lessons. Some of the kids want to work with you again. I told them—" She hesitated, but only for a beat. "I told them you'd be available to teach again for the next six months."

Her words swirled in his head and his gut. His instant joy collided with all the messages saying *No, not you, it'll never work, you're a shitty role model.* He'd loved those kids, and he'd hated himself for not being the man who deserved to teach them. He never wanted to disappoint them like that again.

"No," he said.

She crossed her arms, which was probably supposed to make her look stubborn and tough but mainly made it harder for him not to covet her breasts.

"You can mess with my hair and my clothes, and you can make me go to parties, but this is over the line. That's not my image. That's my life."

A few of the musicians had gone back up front and were messing around, so he couldn't hear what she said next, just watched her lush lips and thought about kissing off all her lipstick. "What?"

She leaned in. He guessed at some level he'd wanted her to. He could smell her perfume, assaulting his senses and traveling every synapse in his brain, right down his spinal cord.

"Not for your image. For *you*. Because you loved it." Her lips were closer to his ear than they had to be, surely. If he could feel warm breath, if he could sense the movement of her mouth, if he could imagine her tongue curling into the crevices of his ear and her teeth nipping his lobe—she was too close.

"Let me make this happen."

Her breath feathered against his skin, a sensation that wound its way through his whole body.

Neither of them said anything and she didn't move. He breathed her, the soft scent of lust under all the perfume, the strongest and best.

She stepped away, taking her warmth and scent with her. Disappointment curled in him. He hadn't really thought that she'd—that anything could happen between them—

He hadn't thought it, but he'd wanted it.

"Okay," he said. Somehow, it felt as if he was agreeing to more than music lessons.

She was straightening her clothes, stiffening her back, putting her whole Haven costume on again. "I'll let you get to it. I didn't mean to take up your whole break."

"No—it was— I'm glad. And thanks."

Don't go.

He didn't just mean physically. He wanted her close to him again, taking him in. She'd seen him. She'd said—

This is you, right?

Because you loved it.

"So, yeah—I'd better go. I'll be in touch about the lessons. And regardless, Wednesday, my office, meeting with Pete."

"Yeah," he said.

She turned away slowly, as though she, too, felt the tension between them and was unwilling to let go.

An arm came around his shoulders from behind. "You want to get back up there?"

He watched her head to her seat, the tight sway of her in those jeans, the perfect compact hourglass of her figure. He could still feel the whisper of warm air across his cheek. An inch and she would have been kissing him.

"She your girlfriend?"

It was Devon, the house band's leader. Mark turned and got blasted with beer breath and a way-too-up-close view of Devon's scruffy beard. Well, that was a serious comedown.

"Nah," Mark said.

"Too bad, huh?"

"Nah. Women like that—"

"More trouble than they're worth?"

Mark nodded, thinking, *I can't afford what she's worth.*

5

SHE SET UP Mark's first guitar lesson for Monday afternoon. It was absurdly easy. She emailed one of his former students, a high schooler who'd been playing guitar for a few years. She had to talk to his mom, too, since she was footing the bill. Haven had expected some pushback from the mother, maybe even some concern about whether Mark was a good influence on her son. Haven had prepared a speech about how Mark had turned his life around. But all the mother said was, "I'm only paying for these lessons if he practices."

It was also surprisingly easy to convince Mark to let her attend the lessons, or at least the first one. "I told Jimmy Jeffers I'd stick to you like glue from this point on," she'd said, and his response had simply been, "I guess there are worse fates." After the night she'd spent watching him play, she wasn't sure whether to take that as resignation or flirtation. She couldn't point to anything that had crossed any line, and yet she had left the club in a state of agitation, her body fizzing, warm, needy. The soap scent of his skin had been bright in her sinuses, her mouth still dry from the charge that leapt between the two of them when she leaned in.

Mark had agreed to meet his student in the high school band room, and the two of them sat now on uncomfortable folding chairs, guitars in their laps. Haven had tried to stay quiet and watch, but her antsiness got the better of her, and she ended up pacing. To take her mind off Mark, she read the posters and brochures tacked up on the walls. But she couldn't calm down or keep from half listening as Mark talked to his student.

Gavin Hecht looked a great deal like Mark had before the first stages of his makeover—long-haired, scruffy, badly dressed. He was also pimply and awkward and scrawny, but damn, for a kid he could play the guitar. And Mark was good with him. Low key, not demanding, man-to-man. Doing more listening than talking, but asking a lot of questions.

Haven pretended to thumb through a book about building a better color guard, but really she was hyperconscious of every move Mark made. He leaned back in his chair, watched Gavin patiently, both the kid's fingers and his face, as if there was so much to learn from this guy that he couldn't tear his eyes away. And yet, every so often his gaze fell on Haven like a touch—on her hair, on the hem of her skirt, on all the parts of her that were alert to him.

Which, for complicated reasons, made her think about her date on Saturday night—two nights after she'd watched Mark jam—with Jewelry Marketing Guy, whose name was Greg. It had been perfect, on paper.

Greg had showed up in a thoroughly pressed blazer, taken her to an art opening, introduced her to people he knew and made smooth small talk with people *she* knew. He took her to dinner, held the door, removed her coat and turned it over to the hostess, pulled out her seat. He told her about his job and listened intently while she talked about hers. And there was something to be said for *not* feeling as though she had a whole Olympic luge team hurtling around in her stomach. She was way more relaxed with this guy than she'd been with Mark, and that seemed to bode well for compatibility. Compatibility, after all, was what she was after.

After a tasty death-by-chocolate dessert, he paid for the dinner without making too big a fuss about it, and he hailed them a cab and took her back to her apartment. In her mental tally, she gave him points for each of those accomplishments, and she decided that she should definitely let him kiss her.

The driver asked if he should wait, and Greg said no, he'd walk home. That was smooth, Haven thought. No cab idling at the curb, but no making it too obvious that he hoped for curbside—or upstairs—action. Another point in the plus column, and none—none!—in the minus column. This was the most promising date she'd had in eons. She couldn't wait to tell Elisa.

The street had been quiet outside her building. "Thank you," she said. "I had a lovely time."

"Me, too," Greg said.

He took a step closer to her and bent to kiss her. It took a long time for his face to get near hers. Was he moving at snail speed? His lips touched hers. Then he drew back and smiled at her.

Huh.

Well, it had been a very brief kiss. Not really long enough to *feel* anything.

For some reason, she thought of Mark's face in the barbershop mirror. That intense gaze, as if he knew exactly what she was wearing under her clothes and, even worse, what she was thinking.

Greg had looked at her closely, as if gauging her reaction, and then lowered his face again.

Kissing her. Like, serious. Not bad technique. Not wet or sloppy or too much tongue or anything negative she could think of. In fact, on paper, this should have been perfect.

It was just that it was *entirely on paper*. Not a molecule of arousal stirred in her.

Whereas on Friday night, watching Mark play guitar, just *talking* to him, it had *all* been stirring. Parts she didn't even know she had, actually, little invisible hairs and supersensitive bits of skin.

Those same parts were stirring now—*Where is he? What is he doing?*—almost as though they were iron filings, straining toward him. If she let down her guard, would she be drawn right over there?

She let herself watch, because it was too hard not to. Mark was explaining something about picking technique, leaning over his gorgeous—almost tiger-striped—acoustic guitar and showing Gavin what he was doing. While Mark was talking, Gavin started strumming and messing around with fingerings, which would have driven Haven crazy—because obviously he wasn't paying attention if he was playing. But Mark didn't make him stop. In fact, Mark stopped playing and talking, and listened to Gavin, with his full, undivided attention.

"Let me show you something," Mark said. He played the same lick, but with embellishments. It made Gavin's rendition sound small and flat, as if Mark's was full of something—emotion, Haven thought—that Gavin hadn't quite managed to reach for.

Gavin played the phrase again. And wow. Not flat any more. The kid had played something almost soulful, and yet not an imitation of what Mark had played. This was very much Gavin's. Mark had heard it in the kid's playing and brought it out of him.

Hell, yeah, there would be more music lessons. And maybe she'd see what else she could set up along these lines. There were organizations, nonprofits and so forth, that helped get music into kids' lives. She'd bet Mark would love that. It wouldn't hurt his image, either.

Huh. That last bit had been an afterthought, not her main focus. *Eyes on the prize, Haven,* she chided herself.

"Thanks, man," Gavin said, and began packing up his guitar.

Even the way Mark shook hands with Gavin, earnestly, seriously, that same man-to-man vibe about it, was perfect.

"What about little kids?" she asked Mark, after Gavin had left and they were alone in the echoey band room. "You like working with them, too?"

She leaned against the piano, keeping her distance from him, as if that would help. As if that would stop the iron filings from aligning to him.

He nodded. "All ages. Any kid that's serious about playing guitar or piano."

"You play piano, too?"

He shrugged. "Enough to give good lessons. Hey, you want me to show you a couple things on the guitar?"

She shook her head. "I'm hopelessly unmusical."

He wrinkled his nose at her, and the almost-smirk of it did something funny to her lower belly. "Nah. I saw you tapping your foot the other night."

Oh, had he? He'd been watching, then, when she didn't know he was. He'd been watching her the same way she'd been watching him.

That revelation showed up as warmth in her chest and heat between her legs and something that swirled on the surface of her skin. She had to get ahold of herself. No good could come of any of this, not the little hairs or the sensitive skin, not the iron filings, not the hyperawareness and not the way he was urging her into one of the uncomfortable chairs and settling the guitar in her lap, wrapping her hand around its neck with warm, strong fingers. Musician fingers. Not just warm and strong, but probably agile, too. Well, hell.

She was disappointed and grateful when he released her hand and let her do it herself.

"Thing is," Mark said thoughtfully, "There's native talent. And that's helpful. But a lot of music is hard work. You can't say you're not musical if you've never put in any work. That's what I mainly try to get across to the kids. I mean, I'm psyched if I teach them something new, and especially if I get them excited. Like I said, the best rush is getting to kids who don't get excited about much. But the other thing is, I try to help them realize that sticking with it and working hard is more important than being some prodigy."

She looked away from her fingers on the guitar's neck and up at his face. His eyes were bright.

"I bet even when you weren't the best role model, you did them more good than harm," she said.

He shrugged. "Who knows? Anyway..." He unfurled one of her fingers and reconnected it with the string. "This is a C chord. First thing everyone learns."

He guided her fingers, then showed her how to strum the chord with her other hand. "How's your dad doing?" she asked, to distract herself from the way his touch had raised goosebumps along her arms.

"He's improving," Mark said. "I've been talking to him almost every day. I think he's lonely."

She caught his eye; his expression was wistful but also pleased. "I bet you cheer him up a lot," she said. "I'm glad you guys have been talking. I know you said you wanted more connection to him."

"I wish it hadn't taken this to make it happen."

"Me, too," she said. "But the important thing is, it's happening, right?"

He readjusted her index finger where it clutched the string to the fingerboard. It hurt, the way the string cut into her flesh, and without thinking, she reached for his hand and turned it over, stroking her thumb across his fingertips. "Calluses," she observed.

He drew an uneven breath and she dropped his hand, aware suddenly that *she'd* crossed a line.

She stood up quickly and handed him the guitar. "I'd better get going." She smoothed her skirt down and checked to make sure no pins were coming out of her hair. Despite the fact that everything was in order, she felt ruffled, as if the uneven thud of her heart were somehow visible.

"Set up more lessons," she told him from the safe distance of the doorway. "Meanwhile, I'll send you some info about nonprofits that have to do with music and kids. We could do some fund-raising work for them— I think that would go a *long* way toward getting your image back on track, and might be something you'd find fun, too."

"Sounds good," he said. He held his guitar by the neck and stared after her. She couldn't read the look on his face.

Well, damn it, she shouldn't be trying to interpret his mysterious looks, anyway.

"Tomorrow. Pete. My office," she said.

And got the hell out of there.

"Mr. Sovereign's here to see you."

Bennie, Haven's receptionist, poked her head into Haven's office.

"Thanks. Send him in."

Haven had purposely asked Pete to come a few minutes before Mark so he wouldn't feel ganged up on. She wanted a few minutes alone to make nice with him, too, and get him in a good frame of mind. She hoped she could soften him up for Mark's apology.

Pete Sovereign was a good-looking guy. He still had the boy-band appeal—clean shaven with longish blond bangs falling in his face and bright green eyes that would have dazzled her if he'd been her type. She came briskly around the desk and put out her hand. "Haven Hoyt."

"Pete Sovereign," he drawled, the Southern accent ringing false, since she knew he was New England born and raised. He had a loping gait that she suspected was put on, too.

She took her hand back. He'd held onto it too long, almost as if he were thinking of leaning down and kissing it. And he was giving her a ton of eye contact, all kinds of dark, stormy and come-hither. Pete Sovereign had an image going on.

She could respect that. He'd figured out what worked for him and stuck with it. The result was a healthy solo musical career, and he was in no hurry to go on the tour because it would mean taking a break from his own work to do it. She was sure it would only be worth it to him if he was convinced they'd make a fortune, and if Mark flaked out on them—

Well, that would mean no fortune for Pete or any of them.

"Mark's on his way." She hoped he was, anyway. She'd called him last night to make sure he wouldn't forget the meeting, and he'd been drunk enough that she could hear it in his voice. She'd told him to quit drinking, slug a quart of water and take two aspirin. She had her fingers crossed that he wasn't passed out or too hungover to move.

"So, hey," she said. "I know things haven't been the easiest between you and Mark, but I want you to know I'm working with him, and we're smoothing out the rough edges."

"I've heard good things about you and your work," Pete said. "Sounds like if anyone knows what to do with rough edges, it's you."

She tried not to let the flattery get under her skin, but she couldn't help blushing.

"I hope Mark hasn't totally poisoned you against me. I'm not *all* bad."

"I always reserve the right to make my own judgments."

"I admire that."

An awkward moment settled on them, and she didn't know what to say next. He didn't fill the silence. Finally she said, "Anyway, I just wanted you to know, Mark and I both really appreciate your willingness to stop by today. Takes a big man to give a guy a second chance, let alone a third. I respect that."

She watched his face carefully for signs she was troweling it on too thick, but he just nodded and got a faint smile on his face. "Well, I mean, no biggie. My pleasure."

"This tour's going to be great," she said. "You guys are going to kick butt and take names."

She'd found it worked well to talk about things she wanted as if they were fait accompli. This put her in the right mindset, and she found it helped her get other people there, too. Sure enough, Pete was still nodding. "Yeah, hell, yeah. We sure will."

"Hav?" It was Bennie again. "Mark Webster."

"Send him in."

"Hey."

Mark barely made eye contact with her, and he didn't acknowledge Pete at all. Not a good start. "Hey, Mark—I was just telling Pete how much I appreciated his willingness to talk this out."

"Yeah."

Jesus. What was she going to do with him? Get this over with as fast as possible before it blew up on her, that's what. And before—before she started thinking about how good he looked. He was wearing camel-colored cords and a soft brown sweater she'd picked out for him. She knew how soft it was, and she'd seen it on him in the dressing room, so she didn't have to stare at his pecs to know how well it fit his shoulders and chest. She thought of Judy's hands tracing Mark's seams, fussing over the line of his clothes, and how much she'd wanted to brush Judy off and put her own hands on him.

She thought of the way his hands had felt on hers, urging her into intimacy with the guitar. She thought of the wistfulness he wore when he talked about his dad.

She thought about the night at Village Blues and those moments when they'd talked. He'd revealed so much of himself to her, and she understood that he couldn't hear his own talent, that he'd made himself sacrifice the music lessons he loved to give. He was only half living his life.

That night he'd smelled tangy, some kind of sea-scented aftershave that made her want to put her fingers in the holes in his jeans, the ones in the knees, the ones where the pockets were stitched to the butt. And the one just opening up from strain alongside his zipper, barely big enough for the tip of her pinky.

She'd thought, *I wish we were alone*, and *Thank God we're not alone*.

"So…" Pete said impatiently, and she jumped.

"Pete—we asked you to come here today because Mark has something he wants to say about the breakup of the band."

"Yeah?"

She didn't like the challenge on Pete's face as he eyed Mark with a slight smirk. What had happened to the charming image he'd trotted out for her? Was he completely two-faced, or did he hate Mark Webster that much? And if so, *why*?

Regardless, she had to get things back on track. "And let me just say again that we appreciate so much your willingness to hear him out."

She could almost see Pete preening at that, the lift in his shoulders and tilt of his chin. What an ego. She just wanted to get this over with. If Mark could issue the apology and Pete would accept it, they could move on. She could get Pete out of the room. While Pete's shoulders had lifted and the corner of a cocky grin had found its way onto his arrogant face, Mark's stance had slumped a few more inches.

If you'd asked her before she'd met him, she would have said she didn't feel sorry for Mark Webster at all.

She believed he'd gotten himself into this fix. Now, though, as she looked at the two men, she had trouble buying that version of events. Something had happened to her during the time she'd spent with Mark—aside from the obvious fact that he lit her hormones on fire. She'd gotten to *like* him.

You'd think it was a good thing, liking your client, but she wasn't so sure. A good criminal lawyer didn't have to believe in his client's innocence to defend him, and a good image consultant didn't have to like her client. It wasn't up to Haven to decide whether someone was worthy of fame. She didn't have to feel as though the old image was ill-deserved and the new one overdue. She just did her job to the best of her abilities.

Right. She had a job. She had to remember that.

"Mark—go ahead."

"I regret any lasting damage my temper has caused you."

Mark said it well. He raised his head, straightened his shoulders and looked Pete in the eye, just as she'd instructed him. She could even hear sincerity in his voice. As far as the apology went, she believed he meant it.

Pete's rogue eyebrow went up farther. She could tell he wasn't fooled. He knew a non-apology when he heard one, but he didn't jump on it. Instead he scrutinized Mark, a cool appraisal that made Haven's blood run cold. "That's very kind of you, Webster."

The hairs on the back of her neck rose, a slow reverse domino effect.

"You should know, I'm leaning heavily toward doing the tour," Pete said.

They were the right words, and she let herself relax a bit.

Her first stupid decision.

Pete's smirk widened a degree. "I could be persuaded quite easily."

"What would it take to persuade you?" Haven asked. She had to keep Pete talking, to move him in the direction of closing this deal. If that meant playing straight man, so be it.

How could one not-particularly-handsome face show so much self-satisfaction? Now that she looked at him up close, he didn't seem boyish as much as just bland. He had none of the hard lines or beautiful bone structure that Mark did. In fact, he struck her as dissipated, soft around the jawline and puffy under the eyes. He'd been living as hard as Mark had, in his own way, and for a moment she felt sorry for both of them. This was the price of early fame.

"Tell you what," Pete said. "Why don't you and I have dinner tomorrow night and I'll let you do your best to convince me."

For a brief moment she failed to understand. She thought he was talking to Mark, and she couldn't figure out why Pete, who clearly hated him, would ask to have dinner with him. And then she got it, and her instincts said a low, firm, *No*.

Actually, it was Mark who'd said no. He'd straightened up to look squarely at Pete, and he said it again. "No. No way."

If the eyebrow rose any higher it would be lost in Pete's bangs. "What's it to you?"

Her whole body rang a warning, and she tried to call Mark off but couldn't catch his eyes, which were focused with laser precision on Pete. "She's not some pawn you can bargain with."

"Huh," said Pete. "I don't recall asking you. I think Haven can speak for herself. Right, Haven? What do you say. Dinner?"

She understood now, all too well, how Mark kept letting Pete rile him up. The guy was a toad, but it was impossible to ignore him. Given that there had been some unintentionally shared woman in their past—God, Pete was brilliant at this.

"Quit it, Sovereign."

"Why, Webster? Is there any reason Haven can't say yes to a date with me?'

"She's seeing someone, right, Haven?"

Well, yes, she supposed she was technically seeing Jewelry Marketing Guy, since she'd agreed to go out with him again. Regardless, there was no way she would agree to dinner with Pete. Quite apart from the fact that she had no desire to give an evening to him, it would only inflame the situation between him and Mark. "Right," she said.

Her office felt close and hot.

Mark's face was dark. Pete's still wore a smirk.

"Well," said Pete, "that's a pity. Because I'm sure if we had just a little time together you could convince me to do the tour. If you change your mind, let me know. You've got my number, right?"

"You're a dick, you know that?" Mark was all bristle.

"Mark, don't," Haven said.

"This is between you and me, jerkoff. Don't bring her into it."

"This has nothing to do with you and me," Pete said coolly, "and everything to do with how very beautiful I find Haven. Don't you agree? Isn't she beautiful?"

"Mark, *no*." She caught his arm again and almost got yanked over as he lunged at Pete. Pete sidestepped them and headed for the door.

"Don't get your undies in a bundle. Haven, I'm free every night this week. You know where to find me." He gave a little toodle-oo wave, and before Mark could wrest himself free and launch a fresh assault, Pete was gone.

6

THAT *ASSHOLE*. That pile of shit, dickwad, lower-than-scum, son-of-a—

Going after Haven that way, treating her like a pawn, treating her like collateral, like something he could bargain with.

"What the *hell*, Mark?"

It took him a moment to realize she wasn't grateful. She was *pissed*.

"Really? Is that what you think the best approach to this situation is? I had it under control. We told him I was seeing someone—"

"And he couldn't fucking leave it alone. He couldn't—"

"You can't keep doing this, Mark. You can't keep reacting to every little thing he does and says to you. You're totally stuck in the last decade. And you're going to shoot yourself in the foot. Hell, you're going to launch a weapon of mass destruction at your foot. How many second chances do you think you're going to get?"

"I—"

He didn't find himself at a loss for words too often, but this was Haven. And he was not rational where she was concerned, apparently. The barbershop, the department store, the blues jam—nope, not rational.

"You act like a guy who has nothing to lose, but that's not how it is, Mark. You told me yourself, you need this tour. You need this money. Think about your dad."

He hadn't been thinking about his dad when Pete was taunting him into yet another stupid reaction, nor of the new batch of hospital bills that had shown up yesterday. He'd been thinking about Haven—the way she listened, the way she noticed. Her breath on his cheek, her whisper in his ear, the smell of her, the all-over satin glorious sheen of her. How much he wanted her in his hands, around his cock, under him.

He didn't want Pete Sovereign to spend one single solitary moment alone in her company.

"I don't want him to touch you."

He'd said it on impulse, without thought, without regard to what those words would feel like, said out loud. For him *or* for her.

She froze, then deflated quickly, the anger leaving her face, her posture softening. Hearing the words, *I don't want him to touch you*, she'd understood what he was trying to say to her: *I don't want anyone* but me *to touch you.*

She was staring at him as if she'd never seen him before, her eyes big, her lower lip soft and full. It was as if she was *begging* to be kissed, although there was something uncertain in her stance, a hesitation he'd glimpsed only a few times before, mostly during those exposed moments in the mirror. Then she'd looked so unlike the woman Haven Hoyt presented to the world, so unlike the woman he knew she desperately wanted him and everyone else to see.

Haven. This was the woman he wanted to touch, to slip inside, to find his way to the heart of.

He acted without thought, taking her mouth with his. He kissed her hard, pressing his way into her as if he owned her, as if she'd given him permission.

She *was* giving him permission. She opened and softened and her whole body yielded to his, fitting against his length, all heat and spark. She whimpered into his mouth, little bursts of sound every time he found a new part of her with his tongue or mapped out another contour of her body with his hands. The tight, satisfying arch of her ass, the nipped-in slimness of her waist, and against his chest, driving him mad, her full curves. He'd have to let go of her mouth to do it, but he could dip his head and slick his tongue over the upper surface of her breast, and it was, he learned, indeed, as smooth as satin.

She's going to make me stop, he kept thinking. *She's going to make me stop.*

But she didn't. Far from it. She wrapped her fingers in his hair, and with her other hand she groped at his waistband, tugging up his sweater, pulling his T-shirt out of his pants, slipping her small, cool palm up his torso, over his abs, up to his chest. Her hand warmed as she stroked his chest and found his nipple with her thumb. She toyed with it, something he'd never thought he liked, until now.

He found himself backing her up against the door of her office, and he didn't realize he'd found her thigh under her skirt until his fingertips reached the top of her thigh-high stocking. Above the squeeze of the elastic, her skin was soft and warm. His cock throbbed, painfully hard against his fly.

Now she's going to make me stop.

She could have made him stop. All she would have to do was flinch or hesitate. Probably she could have cooled his ardor by being merely cooperative, lukewarm.

But there was nothing lukewarm about Haven right now. She squeezed her thighs together, trapping his fingers in the softness there, and he stopped breathing for a second. Stopped moving.

She grabbed his wrist and moved his hand higher.

Holy fuck.

His fingers traced an edge of lace, slipped under, found a fuzz of hair, then her sweet, damp heat. He kissed her again, and her mouth slid against his, her tongue parrying and retreating, flirting, urging. When his fingers touched her opening, she moaned, and he had to brace himself against the wall and take a mental five seconds.

Both her hands were on his fly now, grappling with the button and working the zipper down.

I'm going to fuck her against the door of her office and she's going to let me.

She bit his lip, hard enough to draw blood, and he

pushed her more forcefully against the door, crushing her hands between them. She kissed him harder. The sounds she made were quiet but intense, as if she were aware of her secretary outside but unable to stop what was bubbling up from inside her. It was quite possibly the sexiest thing he'd ever heard.

She's not going to stop me.

He didn't understand. Not completely. Why would a woman like Haven Hoyt let herself do what Haven was doing, let herself lose control, let herself want a man like him? She pressed her pussy against his hand, his middle and index fingers inside her, her clit slick and swollen against his thumb.

"You are the hottest woman I've ever met," he said, because it was the truth and he couldn't help but say it.

Now she had her hand in his briefs, around his cock, and oh, God, what was she doing? Licking her palm and sliding it around the head, slipping down and trapping his cock against his abs. It didn't make sense that Haven, who didn't look like she could tolerate having a hair out of place, was making everything so insanely wet and slippery. He couldn't even catalog it all, the slip-slide of her mouth on his, the slick wetness between her legs, the ease of her hand jacking him higher and higher, almost frictionless with saliva and skill.

She was going to make him come, and he wasn't a hair-trigger kind of guy. He prided himself on his control, on his ability to draw things out and make them good for a woman. But if she didn't stop that, he wouldn't be able to sort out the sensations, catalog them, control them. They were going to consume him and break him open from the inside.

She broke her mouth free of his, suddenly. "I'm coming," she gasped, unnecessarily, because he could feel the spasms against his fingers, feel her hands on his cock become frantic. He wasn't stopping her, she wasn't stopping him, neither of them was stopping this madness, and air hissed from her throat, a silent scream, her face buried against his chest. His orgasm boiled up from his toes, harsh, gripping, almost painful, his cum spilling over her fingers.

For a few moments afterward, he almost believed it would be okay. He was limp with satisfaction and relief, his legs barely holding him up, and he told himself in that moment of starry, stupid bliss that it hadn't been a colossal, braindead, unprofessional—what had she called it?—*weapon of mass destruction to the foot.* That, as out of control as she'd seemed, Haven had actually been in command of herself and had made a decision that she could live with. He hoped she'd lift her head now and smile at him and they'd joke around but also acknowledge the seriousness of the connection they'd forged. This sort of thing didn't happen all the time. You didn't want to do it again three seconds after you were done, not usually, not—

Not ever, if he were honest.

Then she lifted her head, and he saw right away from her face that it was nowhere near okay.

THE LAST TREMOR of the best orgasm of her life had not yet faded when Haven's brain started working again.

Oh, my God, what have I done?

His arms, tight around her, were holding her up. Her legs were too weak to support her.

Standing. For a brief moment her mind was split between horror and admiration. *Standing! We made each other come standing up!* This was accompanied by a reverberation of vivid, intense memory, of the way she'd *needed needed needed needed.* An echo of pleasure, and pure, silver sensation.

Then a flood of shame. *Standing next to my office door.*

With my administrative assistant on the other side. Did she hear?

What kinds of noises did I make?

Haven couldn't remember. Couldn't remember anything she'd done, in fact, or anything she'd thought. All she could remember was how good it had felt and how much she'd *craved* the momentum, the rush, loving the way her need had driven her along, clutching and reaching and grabbing. She'd never felt anything like this before, the slick heat of his mouth and how it had merged in her mind with the hot, wet need between her legs and the feel of his iron-hard cock sliding under her palm—which she had *licked.*

She remembered that part because one of the things she'd never really liked about sex was how messy it was. Why couldn't it be more civilized?

Her hands were covered with his semen, sticky and wet. Shouldn't she be more upset about that? She felt removed from what had happened between them, as if she'd read about it in a book. Had she really loved the way his cock had looked and felt when he'd come all over her hands, definitive proof that she'd made him lose control?

His hands were still on her, his fingers still in her, her body still fluttering against his touch. Damn, he was an expert at that. From the moment he'd touched the lace edge of her panties, she'd known he was going to make her come and she was going to let him.

And, oh, God, that made her remember that she'd been unwaxed and not freshly daubed clean, no newly applied deodorant—and she'd been sweating from the strain of dealing with Pete and Mark. Who *knew* what her breath smelled like, because she'd brushed her teeth this morning, of course, but then there had been her coffee-and-bagel breakfast.

He knew what her breath smelled like. He knew she'd totally and completely lost control of everything—of the situation, of her image, of herself.

The last spasms were subsiding, and her body was cooling. The mess on her hands felt far less like a gift. There was no bathroom inside her office, only the one out there past her admin's desk. In her own desk, she had a roll of paper towels and a box of tissues.

Shame. Regret.

She lifted her head. He was waiting for her, his eyes questioning.

She saw no such negative emotions there, and that made her angry. This wasn't just her loss of control, it was his, too. She wasn't the only one who had something to lose by screwing this up. If anything, he had more.

She pushed his hand out from under her skirt and

broke away from his embrace. Retreating to the desk and using the toe of her shoe, she opened the bottom drawer and extricated the paper towels.

He was watching her, and now he looked worried. *Good.*

Turning her back to him, she cleaned herself up with angry swipes. He should understand that she wasn't one of those women he could pin against an office door without consequences.

She knew she was furious with herself, not with him, but it was impossible to keep the anger fully contained. It was just too big.

She gave him a paper towel.

"Haven."

"We shouldn't have done that."

"Let's talk about it."

"There's nothing to talk *about*."

"It was—"

"It was a mistake."

Even though part of her wanted to know what he'd been going to say. It was what? It was—

It was sordid, unacceptable. And a terrible, unprofessional mistake that she might regret the rest of her life. She was a rising star in image consultation, in the biggest city in the United States. She had celebrity clients and great word of mouth. But she'd skirted close to fiasco with the Celine incident, and the circles she moved in were extremely unforgiving. She competed for work against a small group of high-powered women, including the notorious image consultant clique referred to as the Power Girls, who were ruthless and would dismantle her if she gave them the slightest opportunity. They had friends in the highest of high places and they'd happily smear Haven's own image all over local and national media. The muddle would be just as big as the one she and Mark had just made with their out-of-control lust.

Haven Hoyt. Sex—or what passed for it—with a client. In her office. With her admin in earshot. Who'd want her to rehab an image after *that*?

No one.

She tossed the paper towel, the evidence of their madness, into the trash and dug in her desk, praying for a Wet-Nap. She needed time to think.

Damage control. She was the queen of damage control, right? The queen of image.

There was nothing to fear here. She'd rescued far more sensitive situations from far grubbier human foibles.

She could do this. She could put it back together again.

But not if she looked at Mark. If she let herself see the tenderness on his face full-on, she'd never be able to clean this up.

"First," she said. "This never happened."

"Haven—"

"This. Never. Happened. You have to promise me."

If he couldn't promise, she'd move to the next level. Bribery.

Blackmail came after that, but she'd never had to go there before and she didn't want to start. Her fingers were crossed that he'd be reasonable and she could keep things aboveboard. She prided herself on her ethics, one of the things that differentiated her from some of her sharky competitors. She could clean up a mess without crossing those lines.

"Who would I tell?"

"Pete Sovereign. Jimmy Jeffers. Some buddy you like to brag to. You can't tell *anyone*."

He turned his head away and wiped his fingers on the paper towel. His face was dark now, his expression grim and his mouth twisted.

Her stomach knotted. Why did this feel like grief? She'd extinguished a light in his eyes she'd only caught a few glimpses of. A playfulness, a hopefulness she'd seen in flashes in the barbershop and again in the personal shopper's suite. The night in the blues club. Monday afternoon, working with Gavin.

Surely, though, she wasn't his type any more than he was hers. He needed some woman who would find nothing more entertaining than the dark, close atmosphere of a blues club, someone who understood his music and could talk to him about things she didn't understand— notes and keys and rhythm, art and emotion, soul and depth—a woman like her mother or her sisters.

"I won't tell anyone," he said. "It wouldn't make any sense if I did, anyway."

That was for goddamned sure. She couldn't explain the sexual heat she'd felt when he'd stood up for her against Pete or the rush of longing when he'd said *I don't want him to touch you.*

Insane, fierce *need* that had taken over the second he'd touched her. She'd gone to a place beyond herself, where all sense and sanity had been drowned by *want*.

"But I also don't see what was so bad about it," he said.

"It was wrong. You're my client. And if it got out, it could destroy my career. Image consulting is dog-eat-dog."

He looked down. "And I'm bad for your image."

"Letting a client do—*that*—against my office door with my admin outside, yes, that would be bad for my image."

He shook his head. "*That?* That's what we just did? *That?* Something so dirty and weird you don't even have a name for it?"

"What would you call it?"

"Jesus, Haven."

"Well?"

She wasn't sure why she was goading him. Maybe there was a tiny part of her that wanted him to fight back, to tell her that what had happened was more than she was admitting. Not only *that*, but something else, something he had a name for even if she didn't.

But he didn't answer. Instead he said, "I'm not going to say anything to anyone. And if you don't want it to happen again, it won't."

What if...

What if I do want it to happen again?

It can't, said the voice of reason.

"If it happens again…" She said it as much for her own benefit as for his, because she didn't trust herself any more, not after *that*. "If it happens again, I'll have to drop you as a client."

"No," he said. "No. God knows, I'd walk away from this whole train wreck if I could, but I can't. I got new hospital bills this morning. I thought I had everything, but then I got *$19,000 more*, Hav. Can you believe it? Which means I need your help. So if those are the terms, I get it."

He stuck out his hand.

For a moment she didn't understand what he wanted from her. Then she realized he was waiting for her to shake on it. They were making a deal. No more of *that*, the act with no name that was more than it seemed. All business from this point forward.

She took his hand and shook.

7

ELISA TUCKED HERSELF into the corner of Haven's couch and sipped her red wine. "So," she said. "Tell me about Greg Stoneham."

"He's great," said Haven.

Elisa narrowed her eyes. Haven held up for a moment under her scrutiny, then wilted and sighed. She'd been looking forward to this girls' night, but also dreading it. Since Wednesday evening she'd been able to think of nothing but Mark's mouth on hers and his hand in her panties. If there was anyone on Earth capable of reading her mind, it was Elisa.

"Let me guess. He seems like a great guy, but there's no spark."

Haven bowed her head, guilty as charged. "Am I that predictable?"

"You're pretty predictable."

"I told him I'd go out with him again."

"That was open-minded of you."

"You told me I wasn't allowed to reject them after

one date if I couldn't explain why they weren't right. You said I had to give the chemistry at least a small window to develop."

"Right. Right, I did. Which was very sensible of me. So, when are you guys going out again?"

"Saturday night."

"Could you try to sound at least a little bit excited about it?"

"No," said Haven sadly. She might have been able to maintain a shred of optimism if Mark hadn't turned her inside out. But now there was no more lying to herself. For the first time, she knew what it felt like to want someone so much that her whole body conspired against her better judgment. No matter how many chances she gave Greg Stoneham, he would always be an only-on-paper man.

Elisa frowned. "Haven?"

"Uh-huh?"

"What aren't you telling me?"

Haven hadn't known Elisa very long, but their friendship had developed quickly in the wake of their shared experience in the Caribbean. Since then, they'd started hanging out on the occasional evening, drinking red wine and eating dark chocolate. Haven loved Elisa's no-nonsense attitude, but she did fear her friend's ability to see straight to the truth.

Haven sighed. "I'm getting the Cheetos."

Sometimes, if things were particularly bad for one of them, they supplemented the wine-and-chocolate menu with more serious junk food.

"Uh-oh," said Elisa.

Haven brought the bag back to the couch, along with a stack of paper towels, and fortified herself with one of the Cheetos. She had to eat them one at a time and wipe her fingertips in between because she hated the buildup of orange cheese under her nails. "If I tell you this, you can't tell *anyone*."

"I signed a confidentiality agreement," said Elisa. "That's more than you get with most friends."

Haven smiled. "True."

"Spill." Elisa tipped a handful of Cheetos into her mouth, then brushed her palm against her jeans. That right there was the difference between them. The day Haven wiped orange cheese powder on any article of her clothing would be the day hell froze over.

"I have this client—"

"A male client?" Elisa's eyes had lit up.

Haven nodded. "You sound gleeful."

"Because the way you said 'I have this client' is so different from the way you said, 'He's great' when I asked you about Greg. You said 'He's great' like you were talking about a new kitchen tool that helps you open jars more easily. You said, 'I have this client' like you'd just discovered sex."

Haven bit her lip.

"You just discovered sex!"

"No. I mean, it didn't go that far—"

"How far *did* it go?"

Haven gave up all attempts at dignity, fell back against the couch cushions and moaned.

"Use your words," Elisa teased.

So Haven went back to square one and explained

about Mark Webster, the circumstances of the reunion tour, the barbershop, the department store, the meeting with Pete, Pete's proposition.

"And then…" She trailed off, remembering how frustrated she'd been with Mark for losing control of the situation, of the image she was trying so hard to craft for him—and then she'd done exactly the same thing, only with even worse potential consequences.

"And then?" prompted Elisa.

"He— I…" All Haven could do was blush furiously. The recollection of Mark's assault on her senses was as fresh as it had been two days ago.

"Oh, *my*," said Elisa. "I never thought I'd see the day. Remind me again why this is a problem?"

Haven reached into her handbag, pulled out a copy of *Celeb!* and laid it on the table in front of Elisa. Bennie had given her the magazine shortly after Mark left her office the other day, and it had sealed Haven's conviction that she had to be very, very careful about herself around Mark Webster. For both their sakes.

Elisa smoothed the page down. There, in color, were photographs of Haven and Mark in the barbershop, in the department store and walking up the street, laughing. Haven didn't remember what they had been talking about, and it had surprised her to see how happy they both looked. And it had made her incredibly nervous because Haven didn't remember ever seeing a photograph of herself looking that happy. Worse, she and Mark didn't look at all like an image consultant and her disreputable client. They looked like a couple.

"Oh, my God, he's hot," Elisa said.

Haven's nonchalance failed her, and she collapsed over her own lap and buried her face in her hands. "Yes, yes, he is."

Elisa read the text that appeared alongside the photos. "'We spotted hottie guitarist Mark Webster out and about with one of New York's most desirable image consultants, Haven Hoyt. The two were having a grand old time giving Mark a makeover that included a trim and shave at posh Caruso's barbershop and a new wardrobe, courtesy of Saks Fifth Avenue.'"

"Not courtesy," said Haven glumly. "I wish."

"This doesn't seem so bad. 'One of New York's most desirable!' You go, girl."

"Read the rest."

"'Webster could use some image rehab. His pop band broke up nearly a decade ago after Webster brawled with bandmate Pete Sovereign, and Webster has a DUI and a sex-video scandal under his belt (no pun intended). But is Hoyt the best woman to remake this bad boy? She had to be bailed out recently by Rendezvous Dating's Elisa Henderson when a Caribbean dating–boot camp weekend with Celine Carr went awry. Can these two screwups get it right this time?'"

"Okay," Elisa said. "That's maybe not quite as good. But not catastrophic."

"My job is to make other people look good," Haven said. "If I can't manage my own image, where am I? Last year, Karen Folger went from being the toast of the town to not being able to get a client for love or money after she slept with Rich Demillieu, and he wasn't even technically her client. I can't afford to do something that self-destructive. And we are obviously being watched incredibly closely."

"But not forever, right? You guys can pull off this tour. You can both have your successes. And then, when it's over, you can have each other in every flavor of the Kama Sutra."

"I don't know if that's what I want." Then Haven corrected herself. "I know that's *not* what I want. He's a mess, Lise. *So* not my type. I'd just be using him for sex, but it would never work in real life. I need—"

"You *think* you need," Elisa interjected.

"I *know* I need a guy who can live in my world. And this would always be a weird power thing. I'd be forever telling him what to wear and what to say and how to *be* so I wouldn't feel uncomfortable out in public with him. It wouldn't be fair to him and it wouldn't be fun for me. You've seen couples like that."

"I have," Elisa admitted. "And you've got a point. That's an ugly dynamic."

"I think too highly of him to put him in that predicament."

"I've got two warring halves in my brain," Elisa began. "One wants to say, 'Haven, that kind of attraction doesn't come along every day,' and the other wants to say, 'You're dead right.' Because if I heard another client say what you just said to me, about how you know from day one you'd be trying to remake him—I don't know, I just don't like Pygmalion scenarios, you know? I always hated *My Fair Lady*—I never thought there was anything remotely romantic about it. Even Cinderella makes me uncomfortable. I think people should take each other as they are, and if they can't—well, as much as I hate to say it, you're right, it probably isn't meant to be."

Haven felt a faint whisper of disappointment. Had there been a part of her hoping that Elisa would talk her into Mark? That was just silly, right? Everything, all logic, screamed that he was wrong for her.

Even if he wouldn't hate having to dress to live in her world, he wasn't the kind of guy who could ever be happy there. Mark needed to be with someone like him, whose work was about emotion and meaning. He needed a woman who had unplumbed depths.

In reality, it wouldn't take long for the hot sex to burn itself out. What had happened in her office was a fluke. Life wasn't like that, all hot and messy—it couldn't be. *Her* life couldn't be. And once Mark realized that the inner Haven didn't hold an infinite wellspring of passion, it would be all disappointment for both of them.

She'd been right to hit the brakes and shake on the deal. She needed to be incredibly disciplined about sticking with her decision.

"So, then, the trick is just…how do I not have sex with him on my desk?"

"Did you have sex with him on your desk?" Elisa demanded.

"No," said Haven. "Not exactly."

Elisa crossed her arms and waited, but Haven held firm. Rehashing what had happened would only make it harder to hold onto her resolve.

Elisa thought for a moment. "Even though you pay me to, I don't have all the answers. But it seems like you should start by canceling the date with Mr. Seems Like a Good Guy. It's just going to make you bored and twitchy. Beg off that one, and we'll go back to the database. You need an effective distraction."

Haven sighed. "A distraction sounds good."

But she knew it was going to take one hell of a distraction to get her mind off what Mark Webster had to offer. And even more self-control not to indulge it and make her life—and his—even more of a mess.

HAVEN GAVE MARK a narrow-eyed look that both pissed him off and turned him on. That took some skill.

"Where are your new clothes?" she asked.

They'd met in the shoe department of Nordstrom. He was wearing jeans that, admittedly, had seen better days, another gray T-shirt and a zip-up hoodie. No way he was giving up that hoodie—it was the only thing he'd felt normal in since Haven ran off with his jacket. Which reminded him...

"You have my bomber jacket."

"It's at my place," she said.

"I want it back."

"You don't need it. At least, not until after the tour."

"I don't feel like myself without it."

"Can I help you?"

That was the shoe saleswoman, distracting Haven from Mark's sartorial sins—she hadn't even had time to comment that he'd failed to shave the last two days. Before long, they were on a whirlwind tour of the world of men's shoes, and Mark was tucked into one of the leather benches with a stranger's hands on his feet.

As the saleswoman whipped out her shoe horn and wedged him into another pair, Mark's heel began to hurt. There were four pairs in the yes pile, and—he guessed—twenty discards, stacked precariously high in shoeboxes. Haven kept coming up with new kinds of shoes he needed. He'd never known there was so much subtlety to men's shoes, or that there were so many official names—longwings, toe-cap Oxfords, monk straps, penny loafers. He'd only ever referred to running shoes, dress shoes and casual shoes.

"I'm straight," he murmured to Haven when a pair of gray desert boots joined the to-buy stack.

"I have no doubt about that."

Their eyes met, and she looked away quickly but not before he saw that she, too, was thinking about what had happened between them the other day. Good. If he had to be awake nights, suffering the horniness of the damned, she wasn't going to get off any easier—no pun intended, even if it did send a quick visual through his dirty mind.

Haven's hair was up, tightly restrained in a way that made him desperately wish to free it from its bonds, to see it lying long and thick over her shoulders. He wanted to lift it and kiss her neck, then lean closer and nip into her flesh, flicking his tongue against her skin.

The saleswoman had disappeared, looking for a size twelve and a half. Haven had remarked, without a hint of irony, that he had big feet. Then he'd watched a faint blush come up in her cheeks and known that the double entendre hadn't been lost on her.

"We still need to get you running shoes."

"I *have* running shoes."

"Circa 1999?"

"More like 2008," he said.

"Those aren't healthy for your feet," she said. "Think of this as a required upgrade."

He shook his head but let her pick out running shoes for him to try on.

"Hey. I'm working on a little speaking gig for you," she said, as he relaced the sneakers.

His stomach roiled at the thought of getting up in front of a crowd, and he rolled his eyes. "I don't *speak*. I play music."

"You'll like this."

"I doubt it."

"A ten-minute speech at a fund-raiser on how music can change a kid's life, for an organization that raises money to put instruments in the hands of kids who wouldn't otherwise have access. Next Saturday."

Eagerness burst in him unexpectedly. He could do that. He could tell people how music had changed his life and how he'd seen it change other kids' lives.

She was watching him expectantly, as if she could see inside and knew how he was feeling, both his fear and his sense of opportunity.

"Okay," he said.

She smiled.

Had she known that he'd say yes even before he knew?

"I already told them you'd do it."

"Don't you dare do that ever again," he said, but his heart wasn't in it, and when she raised her eyebrows at him, his mouth quirked against his will. "You're coming with me, right?"

"Of course," she said. "Black tie."

It was just relief he felt at knowing he wasn't going to be on his own at one of those fancy events. No way he was thrilled at the mental picture of Haven in a skimpy cocktail dress and stockings with stiletto heels or at the idea of an evening in her company.

Oh, hell, who was he fooling?

When they'd finished with the shoe shopping, Haven handed over her business credit card on his behalf once again.

"Who's paying for all this?"

"You are, with the tour money."

"That's what I was afraid you were going to say. What's going to happen if we can't convince Pete to get on board?"

"Jimmy Jeffers is going to come after you for a lot of money," Haven said. "But don't worry about that. We're going to convince him."

"I don't have your faith."

"Then you don't know me very well," she said.

I know you made these little helpless, broken noises when you came, he thought. *I know you clutched me hard, like you were drowning and I was the only thing that could save you. I know how good it was to see you lose control and how good it feels to see you put back together again. The rest of the world only sees you like this, all polished and primped and presentable, but I saw you.*

"I guess I don't," he said.

She held out the two shopping bags to him.

He took one in each hand. "This doesn't do much for my masculinity, either."

"Looks great on you. Very metro."

The words didn't matter. It was the sideways tilt of her head as she considered him, the appraisal in her eyes, that made his stomach tighten and his cock grow heavy.

"Come on," she said.

"Where are we going?" he asked, though he would have followed her anywhere at that point.

"Socks and underwear?"

"I don't need socks and underwear."

"Your socks have holes in them."

"Who cares?"

"I care."

She was talking about his underclothes, and his stupid heart should know better than to speed up as if she'd made a confession. "I don't need underwear," he said. Because he couldn't bring himself to say, *I didn't ask you to care.*

"Does your underwear have holes in it?"

"If you want to know the answer to that, you're going to have to do independent research."

He watched with pleasure as color rose in her cheeks.

"Don't do that," she said.

"Do what?"

"Flirt with me." She hurried ahead of him.

In the men's accessories department, she was all business, piling pairs of socks and packages of undershirts and T-shirts in his arms. "I don't wear boxer briefs," he said.

"Now you do," she said.

"Why is that?"

She didn't answer. He decided that if being physical with her was off limits, he was going to cause her to blush a hundred times a day. He was going to make her miss what she'd decided it was impossible for them to have. He was going to go home knowing he'd left her wet and frustrated. If that made him a bad man, he wasn't the least bit sorry for it right now. "Because *you* like them?"

She turned away. "Don't wear the ones with holes anymore."

"I don't have ones with holes."

She glared him into submission. Even that was hot. He was losing his mind.

"Okay, maybe a few with holes."

"Throw them out. And Mark?"

"Yes?"

"I hope you're being…"

She didn't seem to be able to finish the sentence and he felt a surge of victorious pleasure. "What, Haven?"

"Discreet in your affairs," she said.

"Discreet in my affairs," he repeated, mocking. "Like, what are we talking about here? No fingering women against the doors of their offices while their assistants are just outside?"

She crossed her arms and looked away. That gave him pleasure, too. Unsettling Haven Hoyt seemed to have become his new sport.

Of course, now that he knew how to really unsettle her, how to make her whimper and moan, none of this was nearly as satisfying as it should have been.

"For the time being, in the short term, you should be…"

"Celibate?"

"Careful."

He had to swallow a smart-ass comment about how she knew from personal experience how quiet he could be. "In short, *celibate*," he said. "Are you sure this warning comes from professional motives?"

"Jesus, Mark."

"Just curious. Are you telling me this because it's important for my image, or because now that you know what you're missing, you don't want anyone else to—"

"You're an asshole," she said.

"That's what they say," he said airily, but he didn't feel as blithe about it as he sounded. He was beginning to believe that if he hung out with Haven long enough, she'd turn him into who she wanted him to be.

And he wouldn't hate that, as he'd once thought.

He loved being around her, enjoying not just their sharp chemistry constantly tickling his senses, but how smart she was, how funny, how expressive, how intuitively she seemed to *get* him.

He loved who he was around her. She made him feel more like himself than he had since—

Well, certainly since he'd quit giving music lessons. And maybe than he had since he'd signed his name on the Sliding Up contract's dotted line.

He had resisted, so hard, the idea of being remade,

only to discover that she had somehow remade him into himself.

"Mark?"

She ran her slim fingers down the length of a brown leather dress belt. His brain ran riot with fantasies. Her fingers along the length of him. That belt, around her wrists, around his bedpost, her curvy body laid out for him like a gift on his bed. He could imagine her huge eyes as he crawled across the sheets toward her, her body arching in anticipation, working against the restraints.

His balls drew up, his cock hardening fast. He was so screwed.

"Mark?"

For a second he was still inside the fantasy and his name on her lips was a plea. Then he snapped to his senses and clutched the pile of plastic-wrapped boxer briefs before they could slide to the floor.

"Yeah?"

"What happened between you and Pete Sovereign?"

He'd been waiting for this question since Tuesday, and dreading it. "Why?"

"I need to understand because we have to figure out how to make this tour happen. I need to know where the hate comes from, on both your parts, so I can figure out how to get him on board."

Mark sighed. "This isn't a good story to tell you in the underwear department."

"Is there a better place to tell this story?"

He thought about it a moment. "No."

"Then shoot." She pulled a studded belt from the

rack, held it up, accepted his vehement head shake and replaced it.

God, he didn't want to get into this with her, and yet he sort of did. Right there you had the way he felt about Haven. Conflicted and backward, all pent up and ready to spill. "There...was this woman."

"So I gathered," Haven said dryly.

"Her name was Lyn. She was a super-groupie. You know the type? Came to every show, knew every lyric of every song, had all of our life histories memorized. She had a lot of industry connections. She'd been around with a lot of bands, she was connected with labels, she was totally plugged in. She promised me things. She said she could get me a solo album. She said it was practically a done deal. She said—she said—"

Haven's eyes were soft, sympathetic, but he just couldn't get the words out. *She said she was in love with me.* "We were a couple," he finished instead.

"And Pete?"

"We'd kind of had this jokey thing in the past about trying to see who could get a woman into bed first. But I had it in my head that he would be able to see that Lyn wasn't one of those women, that she meant something to me. Problem was, he kept pursuing her, so I went to him and said I—I—cared about her—and he had to lay off her."

"And he slept with her anyway." It wasn't a question. She reached out and touched his shoulder.

He had to pull away, because if the warmth of that touch made it past his T-shirt and into his skin, he wouldn't be able to keep from grabbing her and holding her close.

"I shouldn't have hit him. It was just fodder for all the stories that came out after that, saying I was the one who broke up the band. The truth was, Lyn got Pete a solo album instead of me, and when he left, that was what broke up the band. Neither Pete nor Lyn ever tried to set the story straight. Neither did I, because—I didn't want anyone to think I actually gave a shit. I did confront Lyn, but—"

He broke off. Enough. He'd told her the story, he didn't have to go there, to the deepest store of his humiliation and hurt. "Maybe it's juvenile for me to still hold a grudge, but I know what he did, and that he did it knowing it would hurt me. He's not a man I can bring myself to beg for anything. He's definitely not a man who deserves my respect or even tolerance."

"God," she said. "I'm really sorry. That *sucks*."

She'd stopped browsing through belts. The two of them were just standing there, together in the accessories section, her full attention on him. This was Haven—really hearing him.

"Were you in love with her?"

Trust her to cut through all the bullshit. Trust Haven to ask the one question he least wanted to answer.

Somehow he found himself nodding. "I was naive. An idiot."

"Or not such an idiot," she whispered. "I've read your life history, too. You were brought up by a single dad, pretty poor, the two of you worked your asses off to get you to Berklee so you could realize your musical dreams, and then, blam, before you even know it, you're in this manufactured group, touring all over the country, women throwing themselves at you. But you were just a kid. Nineteen, right? So you were naive. It's not a crime."

He'd never seen it like that. Back then, from inside the mess, he'd felt like the biggest fool to ever grace the stage. He'd always assumed he deserved every knock his ego got.

Had anyone ever listened to him the way Haven did? He wasn't sure. Maybe some people went through life without ever feeling *heard* like this.

"What a crappy place for you to be. With Pete and this tour."

He frowned.

"What?" she asked.

"I got a call from my dad today and he's thinking about moving to New York."

"That's good? Bad?"

"It's good. It's great, actually. Like I mentioned earlier, we've been talking almost every day, and he tells me what's going on and I tell him stuff. Like, I filled him in on how you're doing the image thing and about the barber and the personal shopper."

But not about what had happened in Haven's office—the conversation with Pete. That felt too personal. And certainly not what had happened after.

"I'd like to have him around," Mark said. "I believe in family taking care of family. He doesn't want to be sick and alone, and who can blame him? But it'll cost me a fortune to find a place for him. We're still figuring out if he should move in with me. I mean, it would pretty much be the end of my having any life of my own, given his medical condition and that he has nurses coming in all the time. Or even if I took care of him on my own—I need to find a place for him, or a bigger place for the two of us. But that's expensive, and so's the move itself."

She nodded, sympathy on her face. He wondered that he'd ever, even for a moment, thought she was shallow or cold. Her eyes were full of warmth and understanding. As if she got it, how kowtowing to Pete Sovereign was both the worst and the only thing he could do. "In short, the tour has to happen."

"Yeah," he agreed.

"I'll make it happen."

For a moment he felt the purest relief, because he *believed* her. He knew if she said she'd do it, she'd do it.

And then he realized what she was saying.

"You're not going out with him."

"Just once. I think I can persuade him to cooperate."

It was like an old-fashioned scale, his feelings held in the balance. On one side, the money. On the other, the pointless, irrational protectiveness he felt for her. No, not protectiveness. Possessiveness. Mark closed his eyes. He could picture the expression on Haven's face when she came. Unleashed, free. *His*.

How had this happened? How had he let himself feel this much when she was just doing her job? She might be attracted to him, too, but he couldn't delude himself that there was more to it than that.

"What did Lyn say to you?"

"What?" He'd been so deep in his musings that her question caught him off guard.

"When you confronted her? What did she say to you?"

Compared to all the other things that Lyn and Pete had done to him, the defense she'd made that night was nothing. But for him, those words—

He didn't want to tell Haven. It would open him even more to her, render him that much more vulnerable when it turned out he was alone in his feelings. And yet, he couldn't stop himself from answering. Haven made him want to spill everything.

"She apologized. For her mistake."

"Isn't that good?"

"She said she'd meant the things she'd said to me, but then she'd realized—that I just didn't have the talent to make it on my own."

Even now it stung. He'd seen the regret on Lyn's face, the sincerity of her sorrow at having misjudged him. His sense of his own talent and possibility had shut down. And part of him waited, now, for Haven to look at him with the same regret, the way you looked at someone you'd broken bad but inevitable news to. *The patient may not make it till morning.*

You don't have the talent...

But Haven was shaking her head. "She's wrong. She's just wrong. Maybe she figured out that you're not cut out to be a pop musician, but you already knew that. I heard you play blues, Mark. God. You *play*. You made me *believe*. I went home and bought, like, three blues albums. But you know? I wanted to buy yours.

I wanted to lie on my bed with earbuds in and let you fill up my head. Hell, I wanted to *be* you and know I had that kind of passion in me."

The intimacy of her words shook something loose in his chest, and it moved and rattled and cut off his ability to say anything. But he knew his eyes were full of his gratitude.

"And you're amazing with those music lessons. That kid. Gavin. You know that spell in the Harry Potter movies, where Dumbledore uses his wand to pull thoughts out of his head, the tip of the wand kind of draws this little thought thread right out—?" She gestured. "That's what it's like. Like Gavin has all this music in him and you know how to get it out."

He felt himself warm with pleasure and embarrassment as she spoke. Her praise was like a spell.

"Also," she said, but cut herself off with a shake of her head. "Sorry, I should shut up before I get myself in more trouble."

"What?"

For a moment she wouldn't look at him. Then she slowly lifted her gaze, and he saw a mix of emotions there that matched his: confusion, desire, uncertainty. "The music issue aside," she said, "Lyn's an idiot if she didn't appreciate your other talents."

8

"MY OTHER— OH."

Color rushed into Mark's face, and that was enough to get Haven's blood going, moving hot and fast through her veins, swelling her up with need.

Haven wasn't sure what she was doing, but she wanted something more to happen between them. She wouldn't have brought Wednesday up otherwise. It was sheer provocation.

"Turn around," he said.

"What?"

"Turn around. Walk."

She hesitated.

"Do what I say."

This was a side of Mark she hadn't seen, so bossy and self-possessed. His confidence sent a streak of sensation south, a surge of wet heat that stole her breath. She complied, turning and walking. He was right behind her, she could tell, so close her body reacted as if to a touch. And then his hand *was* on her back, and she didn't know if it was the warmth of his palm or the strength and assurance with which he compelled her that made her heart pound so hard.

She realized where he was leading her. The dressing rooms. "No. You're not serious."

"Oh, hell, yeah, I'm serious."

"Mark, we can't do this again. Not *here*."

"Walk."

It wasn't really even a decision. She hadn't stopped to weigh the consequences of obeying versus disobeying, or the potential disaster that would follow what they were contemplating against the possibility of never knowing what would happen next. She simply walked because that was what her body told her to do. It listened to Mark with absolute attention.

She didn't even look around to see if anyone was watching. She stepped into the dressing rooms ahead of him and felt him draw closer. Then he pushed her through the door, pulled it shut behind them, and pressed her against the wall inside. The wall was cool at her back, his erection hard against her belly.

"I'm going to kiss you." His breath moved past her ear, his words like a touch causing her nipples to tighten.

"Then do it."

"No. I want you to stand here for a minute." His voice was low, dark, husky. "I want you to just stand here and feel what it's like to not be in control of everything, not how you look or how I look or when I'm going to kiss you."

It was hell. It was heaven. She was shaking all over, her panties soaked. Her nipples were over-sensitized, too keenly aware of the rough lace of her bra, yearning for his touch. Each breath felt like effort. The surface of her skin prickled, as if she were packed too tightly with all the sensations, all the emotion, inside her. She ached for more everywhere his body touched hers, and everywhere it didn't. "Please."

"When I'm ready."

He *had* to want it, too. She couldn't be on fire all over without his being affected, at least a little. The power he had over her would be unbearable otherwise.

He started messing with her in other ways, working his palm between her legs gently and slowly to create the perfect friction until she mewled with frustrated desire and tried to press closer. But as soon as she did, he drew back.

Then he lifted a hand and cupped her breast. Just cupped it and didn't touch the sensitive drawn-up tip that yearned for him. This was the worst possible torture. She tried to move to position her nipple against his palm, but again he withdrew the contact as soon as she reached for him. She whimpered.

"I love the noises you make."

She clamped her mouth shut.

"Don't you dare stop."

"I don't think I could," she confessed.

As a reward, he stroked his thumb across her nipple through her blouse, sliding it back and forth, sending streaks of heat and light straight between her legs. The ache she felt became a fierce craving for him. She needed more. She strained for his thigh, and he gave it to her for just a moment, long enough that she could rub frantically against him, withdrawing before she reached fever pitch.

Then he kissed her, as if he couldn't help himself, as if he wanted to consume her, and for a second the heat and twisting and rising sensations in her spiraled so fast she thought she was going to lose control. He stepped back and gave her a devilish, knowing smile.

"More?"

"More."

"You got it."

He knelt.

Oh, God, he couldn't be serious. It was one thing to kiss and grope in a dressing room, and quite another to do what he was so apparently about to do. She'd have to stop wearing skirts. She was making this far too easy for both of them to break her rules. She shouldn't be doing this. She shouldn't be here. She'd told Elisa exactly why this could lead nowhere good.

He put one hand on each thigh and pushed her skirt up.

She clamped her thighs together, and said, "We shouldn't." But the truth was, that only sharpened the sensation, and she had to release the tension or risk coming right then and there.

He pressed his nose against her purple lace panties and breathed deeply. "You smell amazing."

"I can't. You can't."

But he was licking her through the lace, and she could feel the heat of his breath, the dampness of his tongue and the perfect pressure against her clit.

"You don't want to do that," she insisted.

"Do what?"

"What you're doing."

"Oh, believe me, I want to do what I'm doing. And way more." He hooked his fingers into her panties and began sliding them down.

"I didn't… I'm not… I should have…"

But as his thumbs stroked her lips gently apart and his tongue settled against her clit, it didn't seem to bother him in the slightest that she hadn't waxed this week, that she hadn't shaved her thighs this morning, that the smell of her was rising all around them, rich and terrifying, because she had no idea she could be this wet, this messy, this exposed.

She'd had no idea that it could feel this good.

There was the flat of his tongue, hot and everywhere. The grit of his stubble against her skin. The tip of his tongue finding the most sensitive part of her clit and working it over and over again. His tongue swirling, moving around and in until she lost her sense of direction and her knees buckled. His hands gripped her thighs and her ass, holding her up, making sure she didn't fall, while sensation pulled itself together into the tightest knot and burst outward, bright and violent and mind-blowing.

He sat on the chair in the dressing room and drew her down into his lap, until everything made sense again and cold shame found its grip. She wanted to get up and put herself back together, but he wouldn't let her. He held her too tight, his face pressed into her neck, and she couldn't move because her brain wasn't in charge. Her body was content never to be let go.

WHEN SHE CAME, a new surge of wetness on his tongue, he almost lost it too, kneeling there. There'd been no contact on his cock beyond the tight constraint of jeans. Even with no hands, no mouth, no pussy, the over-whelming pleasure and—yes—joy of making her fly apart was almost enough. It was as if he'd somehow lost track of whose body was whose and everything was interchangeable. When her body tensed with sensation and pleasure, his did too.

He just barely managed not to come, and he was glad, because he'd wanted that to be all for her. And now that she was settled limp in his lap, he wanted to give it to her again, right now.

But first, he had an important question for her.

"What was it you were saying before, Hav? You should have...what?"

She lifted her head as if it took a great deal of effort to do so. "It doesn't matter."

"It matters to me. You were going to say something. I want to know what."

She shifted as if she meant to get up, and he pulled her tight against him to keep her from escaping. He knew she wanted to flee. Hell, he even understood her reasons. What they'd just done was idiocy. But he'd given up resisting and he would make her give up, too, if it killed him.

"I just— I wasn't ready."

He looked at her in astonishment.

"No, not like that," she said, flushing. "I mean, I usually..."

She clamped her mouth shut, her face flaming red.

"You're just going to have to say it," he said, "because I have no prayer of getting this one."

"I usually wax. Down there." She said it quickly, without looking at him, obviously dying of embarrassment. "I don't actually usually do *that* at all. I mean, let anyone do that. But if I do, it's only if I'm—smooth."

He was a little stunned. He'd guessed it was hard for her to let go, but he hadn't quite imagined this. "So you've never let anyone go down on you before when you've had…hair?"

"Nope."

"But other stuff is okay. Sex."

She shook her head, the blush deepening.

"Wait a second."

"I like to be *neat*," she said.

"I get neat, but—how do you even accomplish that?"

"If I have a date, and it's like the third or fourth, you know, a crucial date, I just make sure beforehand…"

"And if for some reason you find yourself in a situation where you haven't had a chance to plan ahead?"

"That never happens," she said.

"That never happens," he repeated.

"I wouldn't ever let it happen. I'd make some excuse, or—I don't know."

He was genuinely staggered, and then the implication of her words fully dawned. "But you did. Twice. With me."

"I know," she said, ducking her head again. "I know."

He was flattered. Or honored. More than that. Moved. Moved that not once, but twice, she'd been so—what?—carried away or in the moment or just *with* him that she would break her own hard-and-fast rule. His chest ached, and he wrapped her tighter in his arms and kissed her hair, her ear and her cheek.

Something occurred to him. "What else?" he asked.

"What do you mean?"

"What are the other rules? What else do you have to do before it's okay for you to have sex?"

When she shifted, he loosened his arms and she got up. She slipped her panties on, tugged her skirt down and examined herself in the mirror. As she tucked hair back into place, and rubbed at smeared eye makeup, he couldn't help but think she was putting herself back together so he could take her apart again when they were ready.

His cock responded predictably and he decided he probably was always going to be ready for Haven. As many times as she polished and primped and restored her pristine condition, he'd be there to dismantle her. As long as she'd let him, that was. He was surprised she hadn't started laying down the law yet. Hadn't told him this was the last, last, last time and he'd better not say a word to anyone, et cetera.

He was ready to fight her on it.

After a few moment's silence, she said, "Apartment has to be clean." That same quick, almost ashamed way she'd admitted to not ever having unwaxed oral.

He was the one watching her from behind in the mirror, this time. He could tell she didn't want to make eye contact with him when she confessed to this part of herself. He saw her make the decision to do it anyway, the moment when her gaze came up, and her eyes met his. He felt a click of recognition between them, a sense of something in him settling in deeper and making itself comfortable.

"Sheets have to be fresh."

She was relaxing a little, now, not so stiff and short with her words. He hadn't mocked her, and he guessed that was helping her get used to the idea of telling him this stuff.

"Does it always have to be in bed?"

"It always is."

So that was something else she had given him, her office, this dressing room. Only he had experienced these things with her. His chest clenched again. "I assume hair, makeup, teeth, nails—all done?"

She nodded. There was something on her face. Not pride. Shame. Some pain he didn't, couldn't yet, understand. "It's weird, right?" Her voice was barely above a whisper.

"Not any weirder than anything else." He said it to reassure her, but he meant it. "Not any weirder than how much of a charge I get out of knowing people might hear us, or walk in on us. Right? Sex is weird. You need what you need, for the reasons you need it. And sometimes your body and that deep-down back part of your brain know what that is before your smarter self knows."

Her gaze hadn't left his the whole time he'd been talking, and now her eyes were bright. She opened her mouth, struggled to say something, failed. She put her fingertips to her mouth as though something pained her.

"Look," he said. "I don't care. Body hair, no body hair, clean apartment, ants crawling on yesterday's cereal bowls, I don't give a crap. I like you. I want to be with you. I want you to be comfortable. That's what matters to me."

Her breath caught with a sound suspiciously like a sob. But of course, Haven Hoyt didn't cry. The idea of Haven crying was far more absurd than the idea of her having semipublic sex.

"That's the thing," she said. "I am comfortable with you. I've always cared before, about all the stuff I said— the grooming and the cleaning—but I don't care now. I don't even understand why I stopped caring. All this, all this stuff—" Her voice broke, but she steadied it and went on, "What's happened between us, this isn't like anything I've ever done. I've never been willing to be like this."

She made a gesture that encompassed both of them, the dressing room and something more, something bigger than his going down on her in a department store. And he wanted to know what that was, what it meant to her, but mostly he just wanted to keep feeling the way he felt right now—glad he and Haven were locked in this dressing room together doing probably career-killing things to each other. Thrilled she'd let him see her messy, let him *make* her messy—twice. He was grateful she'd told him why it was hard for her, and that for whatever strange reason, it wasn't as hard for her *with him*.

"Haven," he said.

"Yeah?"

"Is your apartment clean?"

"No."

"Are your sheets clean?"

"No."

"Can we go there? And have sex in your bed? Or maybe even not in your bed?"

She hesitated, but only for a second. Then she turned around and met his gaze. Her eyes were dark and full of feeling. And she nodded.

9

WHAT HAD SHE DONE? What was she doing?

She knew now that she'd been wrong, and hurtful, to reduce what had happened between them in her office to *"that."* She knew it wasn't just about bodies colliding. There was something at work here that she couldn't— or didn't want to—give a name to.

But that didn't mean it wouldn't ruin her.

It didn't mean it wouldn't rob Mark and his father of money they needed.

It didn't mean they wouldn't break each other's hearts when it turned out he didn't want to live the life she'd chosen.

What they were doing now would have consequences. She couldn't see all the ripples yet, but she could feel them. Something as seismic as Mark couldn't happen to her without there being aftershocks.

And yet, here they were in a cab, side by side, on their way to her apartment. She had told him the most naked truth about herself, and she was going to make herself even more naked—maybe completely naked—in just a few minutes.

The craziest part was, there was still time to call it off, but she had no intention of doing so.

"There are dishes on my counter."

"I don't care," he said.

"There's toothpaste in my bathroom sink."

"I find that endearing."

"There's a book of erotic stories and a vibrator on my nightstand."

"Okay, now that's just unfair. I need to know more. What exactly were you doing with this book of erotic stories and vibrator?"

The taxicab driver's eyes found hers in the rearview mirror. "I think that story is going to have to wait," she said, gesturing at the front seat.

"You could whisper."

So she did. "I like to lie on my stomach on the bed and read. And the rule is, I can't touch myself. Not even through my clothes."

"Oh, *God*," Mark groaned. "I shouldn't have asked."

She was glad he'd asked. Telling him, watching his jaw tighten and his color rise, was a total turn-on. She'd never talked like this to anyone, let alone in the back of a cab. She kept such a tight rein on how she presented herself to the world, even with people who didn't have the power to make anything of what they knew.

"Then when I totally can't stand it anymore, when I'm ready to explode, I tease myself with the vibrator. It's not super strong, just a buzz, and I bring it just close enough so I can feel the vibrations, but only that close."

His hand went—involuntarily, she thought—to the bulge in his jeans, and he pressed his palm there, which didn't cool her ardor any. She glanced at the driver, but if he knew what was going on in the backseat of his cab, he was discreetly pretending not to. "God, that's hot," Mark growled.

"I make it last as long as I can. I draw it out, and I make myself watch the clock to see how long I can hold out before I come."

He choked out an incoherent sound, and she reached for the rise of his cock under his jeans. Brushing his hand aside, she found him with the ball of her hand and ground down. She knew the driver might see, and that if the cab stopped, someone could look in. She knew that it would make a mess and that at least one of them would be out of control.

"Hav."

She wasn't sure whether he was imploring her to be sensible or begging her for more. She didn't care. Touching him like this filled her with a sense of power and joy. She wanted to make him feel the way he'd made her feel in the dressing room.

He lifted his hips to her palm and she pressed back, using her thumb to find more topography, the swell of his head, the ridge of vein. He made a nearly inaudible strangled sound. Not "stop."

She checked the mirror, but the cab driver seemed to be keeping his eyes on the road. Her free hand wandered the tightness of the muscles in Mark's thighs and abs. She loved the way his whole body strained in toward the spot she was pleasuring, the way everything got thicker and harder. His face was tight, too, his jaw locked, his eyes now closed. He looked as if he was on the edge, and she felt an answering sensation, like she was poised, like she could follow him right over without a touch, right here in the cab. How had she gotten so plugged in to him that just watching his rising arousal could wind her up like this? It felt amazing and terrible—dangerous and unstoppable.

The cab pulled up in front of her apartment.

She swiped her credit card and they practically fell out of the backseat in their haste to get into the building.

"Ms. Hoyt," said her doorman, with his usual polite nod.

Haven nodded back. "Gerome. On the off chance that anyone asks, you didn't see me with anyone."

"Certainly not, ma'am."

The elevator door had not quite closed when Mark leaned against the wall and lifted Haven up. She wrapped her legs around him, his erection pressed perfectly where she wanted it, hard heat against the part of her that had not stopped aching in days. He kissed her, an open-mouthed, helplessly hungry kiss that made her groan into his mouth and clutch at him. She yanked on his hair, hard enough that he yelped, and then she bit his lip.

A ping announced her floor, and he set her down and followed her out. "Do you do that all the time?" he asked.

"Kiss in elevators? You know I don't."

"Were we kissing? It felt like having sex with all our

clothes on. But no, I meant, do you tell your doorman to be discreet?"

"There's never really been anything I needed him to be discreet about before," she said. "But I have told clients' doormen to be discreet."

"Does it work?"

"I doubt it. But I'd be remiss in not asking."

She unlocked her door and he crowded her into the apartment.

There were shoes scattered around the entry, and she needed to vacuum up dust bunnies here and there. And she couldn't remember whether she'd left chaos in the kitchen and the bathroom—

But he clearly didn't care because as soon as the door closed behind him he scooped her up. Cradling her in his arms he said, "Which way to the bedroom?"

"Straight, first left."

He deposited her on the unmade bed, and she tried not to notice the mess. The underwear she hadn't thrown in the hamper, the clothes hanging off chairs and doorknobs. The sheets themselves, twisted because she hadn't had a good night's sleep since the first time Mark had looked at her in the mirror. She'd dreamed of him, and masturbated to her memories and fantasies of him, and lain awake thinking of what she wanted him to do to her. She'd worried what a terrible, terrible idea it would be to let him.

But now she was letting him, and it did not feel like a terrible idea. It felt like the best idea she'd ever had.

"These sheets," he said. "I love these sheets now that I know what you do in them. They are the dirtiest, filthiest, most awesome sheets in the entire universe and I want to rub them all over my body. You can't ever wash them again. In fact, you can't ever make the bed again."

She laughed even though she actually wanted to cry. He took something that was difficult for her and made it magical and sexy.

She wanted to give him a gift in return. "Sometimes instead of using the vibrator I lie on my stomach and shove the sheets between my legs and rub off on them."

The stuff coming out of her mouth today—she would not have believed it if someone had told her yesterday that she'd be saying those things to him. She would not have believed herself capable of it—with not even a twinge of shame. The only twinge was the one she felt between her legs every time she said something dirty to him. And twinge was too mild a description for what it felt like. The sensation was fierce and hot. Open, and opening still, unfurling, making way for him, not just physically. She wanted more of him in her world, this confusing man who had burst into her life and unmade all her best intentions.

"Show me," he said. "Show me what you do. Show me everything you do."

She stared at him, uncertain.

"Take your hair down."

She would never have picked herself as someone who wanted to be commanded. The loss of control was something she thought would terrify her, but the sensation of yielding to him was as welcome and explicitly sexual as his hand between her legs had been Wednesday. As his mouth had been earlier today. Far from adding restraint, it made her feel released.

She pulled out pins and unwound an elastic, and her hair tumbled down. He ran his hands through it and buried his face in it, and she laughed.

He wasn't laughing as he pulled back. "Take your clothes off."

This was harder. This was nakedness. Real nakedness and more to come. She was certain that the longer she let this go on, the more thoroughly he'd peel away her defenses and get under her skin.

She knelt on the bed, unbuttoned her blouse and let it fall open. His gaze fell to her breasts and stayed there, hot and admiring. She basked in his stare, then shrugged her blouse off. She grew suddenly self-conscious and sucked in her stomach.

"Don't," he said. "Don't hide from me."

"I was just—"

"I won't let you. Now your bra."

She unhooked it with one hand and let it drop. His pupils dilated so fast she saw his eyes darken with it.

He crawled across the bed toward her and did what he'd done earlier, placing a hand on her breast a hair's breadth from her nipple. Her sex tightened and tingled, answering the tautness of her breast. She felt empty in a way only he could fix. But right now he wasn't interested in fixing it, he was interested in teasing. In making the emptiness and the craving grow.

He took her nipple between his thumb and forefinger so lightly she could barely feel him.

"Mmph."

"What do you want?"

"More."

"Like this?" He tightened his fingers infinitesimally, just enough to send a zing of sensation to her clit.

"More."

Tighter.

He lifted his other hand to the other breast. "Does it feel twice as good if I do it to both?"

It felt more than twice as good, some kind of crazy logarithmic multiplier. She wriggled in his fingers, trying to get more touch, more sensation, but whenever she moved, he released her.

"If you want more you have to hold still."

It was supreme torture, with one nipple in each set of clamping fingers, slowly tightening, but if she squirmed or arched or made noise, he stepped it back. She made herself hold completely still until the pressure was exactly, perfectly right, and then she said, "Please, just like that," and he obeyed.

"I'm going to come," she cried, tipping her head back.

"Not yet." He let her go, and the orgasm, which had felt inevitable, retreated. "Skirt."

She unzipped her skirt and lifted herself off the bed to slide it down.

"Lie back. Spread your legs."

She did and he hooked a finger in her panties to sweep them aside.

"Didn't get to really *look* before," he explained. "You're so wet, you're glistening." And he played with a finger in her wetness to show her.

"Nngha."

"You're supposed to be showing me, I know, but I can't not touch. Do you mind?"

She shook her head, officially speechless.

He put the tip of one finger to her clit, and sensation spread like fire all through her groin, gathered itself faster than she thought possible and burst outward. He slid two fingers into her as she came and crooked them upward to tap her G-spot, and she came again, no space between to catch her breath. When her body stopped seizing and convulsing, she discovered both her calves were cramped. She had to take deep breaths to let go.

Then he stood up and took off his sweatshirt and his T-shirt.

This was for her. No mirrors, no Judy. No barber shop, no department store, no clothes.

Just the two of them, and she got to stare at him for as long as she wanted. All the muscles in his torso seemed to narrow toward his waist. Her gaze played over the ridges of his abs, the sculpted perfection of his pecs and the line of muscle that started at his hip and dived downward. The tufts of hair under his arms, the thickness of his shoulders and the leanness of his arms intoxicated her.

Slowly, reverently, she rose to her knees and came to the edge of the bed. He stood there and let her touch, her hands drifting, squeezing, caressing. She followed lines to where they curved, curves to where they ran straight and strong. He was like a cover model in a magazine, but warm and supple to the touch, *real*. Even his hair was just right, dusted across his chest and arrowing down into his jeans.

She reached for the button and he let her unfasten and unzip him. She ducked her head and—

"Nope." He stopped her from putting her mouth where it desperately wanted to go.

She slanted him a look of disbelief.

"I can give you about three minutes, max, Hav. All depends on where you want me."

She groaned. Everywhere. She wanted him everywhere.

"How's this for a deal? You let me inside you now, I'll let you suck me as long as you want later."

There was nothing left to say. She pointed to the night table drawer and he opened it and took out a condom. Tearing the plastic wrapper and dropping it on the floor, he worked the latex down over his cock with one hand. The sight of that hand moving skillfully over his erection made her groan again. He was thicker around than any man she'd been with, cut and perfectly formed, with a wide swollen head she wanted against her soft palate almost more than she wanted him inside her. But not quite.

He slid her panties off and tossed them over the side of the bed. Up toward her he crawled, but this time he insinuated his body between her thighs, letting her feel all of him—the rough chest hair, the ridges of his abs, the trail of hair tickling her clit where her legs had parted wide for him. Then the hard, hot length of him pressing into her, dipping just the very tip into her wetness and—*Jesus*, he was way too good at this—using that same tip to rub back and forth over her too-swollen, too-sensitive clit until she was begging him. *Begging him.* Legs spread, stubble under her arms, breath of unknown freshness, in all her unkempt, unpolished glory, not giving the slightest fuck, saying, "Mark, please, please, please, please, please, please."

Despite what Lyn had done to him, he'd never seen sex as a power game. Sex, especially since Lyn, had been a convenience, a way of forgetting. A way of leaving the things he *didn't* want to think about for a realm where thought was inconvenient and unnecessary.

But between Haven's legs he felt powerful. Hearing the slick, wet sound of her as he moved the head of his cock over her clit, feeling her tipped-up hips pleading with his body to deliver on its promise. And his name on her lips, that *please* like a chant, like a *mantra.* He felt invincible.

"What do you want?" he asked.

She licked her lips, closed her eyes and lifted her hips higher, trying to engage.

He resisted for a moment longer, wanting to prolong this perfect, on-the-edge feeling.

"You're *killing* me," she whispered.

He braced himself on his arms, fitted himself to her without needing a hand to guide him, and gave her the head of his cock. Her heat enveloped him, squeezing him, and his balls drew up tight.

It was too much. He couldn't hold back. He thrust into her abruptly, and she exhaled, a deep half-moan on her lips as she grabbed his ass and pulled him in close.

"Oh," she said. Just that. *Oh.*

He wanted to stay where he was, pressed up against her where she needed him. He wanted to do this for her, let her keep wriggling against him, making little needy, whimpering noises, digging her fingernails into his back and her teeth into his shoulder. He wanted her to come for the fourth time, but he was too far gone. His abs contracted and his hips thrust forward, driving him into her, drawing him back so he could get more— more power, more length, more stroke, more Haven, more, more, more.

And far from complaining, she was crying out her pleasure at the pinnacle of each plunge, his name, *please, more, oh, I'm coming again,* and he wasn't sure he'd given her the three minutes he'd promised her, but there was no helping it now, tension gathering in every muscle in his body, in the curl of his toes and the kinks in his fingers and the strain in his neck, coalescing into something pinpoint small and infinitely big, exploding outward and collapsing inward at the same moment.

He barely had enough of his wits about him to disengage and rescue the condom before he collapsed limply beside her.

She rolled to her side and draped her arm and half her body over him, rested her cheek against his damp chest and sighed contentedly.

Of all of it, of everything, it was that sigh that undid him. Her little exhalation was yielding, was release. He'd made Haven come spectacularly, over and over. He'd made her do things she'd never done before. She'd pushed him beyond his own controls.

But it was the way she willingly put her clean cheek to his sweaty skin and gave herself over to him that choked him up.

And terrified him.

What happens now?

He stroked her hair and listened as her breathing evened and slowed until he was pretty sure she was asleep.

He tried to imagine it. Haven waking up and smiling at him. Telling him, *That was amazing. Let's do it again.*

They'd do it again, Haven just as wild and uninhibited.

They'd order takeout and sit up in her bed—

He was ninety-nine percent sure Haven didn't eat takeout in bed.

He was ninety-nine percent sure Haven wasn't going to smile at him and say, *That was amazing. Let's do it again.*

He had a vivid mental picture of what she'd do when she woke up and found herself twisted in damp sheets, wrapped around his body, salty from sweat that had cooled and dried. She'd pull back and try to smile. She'd reach up and fix her hair into a perfect do, hard and tight, fasten it so it couldn't escape. Then she'd button herself back into her clothes, as if she were putting armor on. And all the while, she wouldn't *quite* look at him, as if by avoiding him she could also avoid having to admit what she was doing, that she was shutting him out and saying goodbye.

He could see it so clearly, it already hurt.

10

IT WAS DARK when Haven woke up, only a little light filtering in from the street, and she didn't know what time it was or why her body was sore all over, her neck stiff, her cheek sticky. And then everything came back.

Her first impulse was to run.

Right now, she felt as if she had something to give him, but that would change. The meeting—colliding, really, a kind of physical cataclysm—of their bodies was enough for him. *For now.*

But eventually he would want to dig deeper. He would want the kind of meeting of souls that someone with his depth deserved. He was filled with emotion and passion, and he was able to find a matching passion in other people, with his music, with his teaching.

And she—

She wouldn't be enough.

But, of course, there was nowhere to run to. He was asleep in her bed.

Her second impulse was to kick him out, but then

she looked at him and found she couldn't take her eyes off him. He was sound asleep, his mouth open just a little, breathing slowly, his long lashes motionless on his beautiful face. Effort and the humidity of the room had curled his hair just a little. He looked so peaceful, almost angelic. She didn't want to wake him. In fact, she didn't want him to go. She wanted to hold onto him as long as she could, as long as he'd have her. But she knew what would come—eventually he'd see that when he cracked her open, he wouldn't find the hidden depths he needed, but only more of what she'd already given him.

So she lay back down, her face on his chest, wrapped her arms around him and went back to sleep.

The next time she woke, it was morning, and he was not in bed with her. A moment of panic set in. He had run. He had kicked *himself* out.

But no, she could hear him moving around the kitchen, and then she could smell coffee and breakfast cooking.

She got up, wrapped herself in a satin robe and went into the kitchen where he was frying eggs wearing only his jeans, slung low on his hips, that fine angled line of hip muscle just visible. He smiled tentatively at her, and she smiled back.

With a quizzical look, as if she hadn't done what he expected her to do, he crossed the kitchen and embraced her. He was warm and solid and somehow fierce. She rested her cheek against his bare skin, his chest hair rough, the now familiar scent of his skin overwhelming her. Her lips almost twitched with how much they wanted to explore his firm contours.

"I wish I were actually a songwriter," he said against her hair. "Because I could write a really good song about that sex."

"Can I ask you a question?" She had to pull away from him a little, because she knew this wasn't an easy question, and it felt like cheating to have her face buried in his chest.

"Anything you want."

"Why'd you do it? Let that producer convince you to play with Sliding Up? Was it really just that you were broke and needed money?"

He turned away, giving the eggs and bacon more attention than they probably required.

"You don't have to answer if you don't want," she said. "I just thought—it seems so far from who you are. Maybe so far from who you *ever* were. I mean, I didn't know you then, and maybe you were really different, but I feel like —" She stopped.

"Like you know me now?" he said.

"I guess I feel like I do."

"I feel like you do, too."

He caught her gaze and held it, and she felt heat wash upward through her body and sweep down again. Behind the heat was something, too, some emotion that filled her and swelled her heart, making it hard for her to keep looking at him.

He crossed his arms protectively. "I guess—I guess I did it because I wanted someone to convince me that the music mattered. It's pretty thankless, you know, being a musician. You work your butt off, you pour your soul into it, and you're lucky if you have an audience, and then you're lucky if the audience enjoys themselves. And these guys came to me and they said, hey, we can make you famous and rich, and you'll have an audience every night, and they'll show up and clap and throw themselves at you. And maybe it was just too much for me to resist."

He flipped the cooked eggs onto two plates, not quite meeting her eye. The lines on his face looked more pronounced, making him seem suddenly old again, the way he'd appeared that first day in the restaurant. She hadn't realized how carefree he'd become with her recently. She thought of the man in the restaurant, how angry and worn-out he'd been.

"It's nothing to be ashamed of," she said.

"I sold out," he said quietly. "I sold out my music."

His voice cracked with the pain of it, and she felt it in herself, like a line fissuring through her own chest. She wanted to do something, anything, to give back to him what he felt he'd lost. He'd made a very human decision all those years ago to be recognized for his work.

"It's not finite," she said. "It's still in you. I heard it the other night. It's not something you sell out and then it's all gone. It's still there for you if you want it. If you wanted to make the blues thing happen, I am totally convinced you could."

He let out a breath then, as if he'd been holding it, all the time they'd been talking. All the time she'd known him, maybe. Maybe all his life. He'd been waiting for someone to absolve him.

He took her in his arms and kissed her so fully and so deeply that she almost said, "Forget breakfast," so she could take him back to bed. But then her phone buzzed and she pulled back, pretending she hadn't seen the look on his face—still quizzical, but now disappointed. The beginning of the deeper disappointment he would feel in her one day not too far off. She went in search of her phone, finding it in her purse on the floor of the bedroom. She wasn't sure how it had failed to wake her up, because she seemed to have twenty-two new voice mails.

There was no way that could be good.

She started to panic almost right away, her mind searching for explanations—something had happened to her family, someone had seen her groping Mark in the cab, someone had released video of their exploits in the dressing room to the press.

"I have to listen to my voice mail," she called to the kitchen. "I have a million messages, apparently, and I only have that many when there's a crisis. Since you're my biggest client, that means the crisis is very likely to be you."

"Haven," the first message began. It was a stranger, and at least there was no death or urgency in the woman's voice. "This is Suellen Marvel at *High Note* magazine. We know Sliding Up is planning a comeback tour, and we'd like to talk to you and set up an interview with Mark Webster."

All the other voice mails were variations on that one. Damn it. They'd lost control of the timing of announcing the tour. Someone—she suspected Jimmy Jeffers, though she knew better than to accuse him—had leaked word of the possible tour to the media. She bet Jimmy had gotten tired of his stars squabbling, tired of waiting for Mark to capitulate and Pete to act like a human being. She bet this was his way of forcing their hands.

All the reporters who'd called her seemed to know that Pete Sovereign was a wild card, that his participation wasn't yet ensured. Some were dubious that he could be convinced, and a few even said they didn't believe that Pete and Mark could ever work together again. Many of them seemed to question her ability to make Mark Webster show-ready, and two mentioned Celine Carr's Caribbean high jinks, doubting flat-out Haven's ability to keep a PR situation from turning into a circus.

Well, they could shove it, because she didn't doubt her abilities.

Except that—

What had she done?

If sleeping with her client wasn't turning a situation into a circus, she had no idea what was.

A total of seventeen separate reporters had contacted her. But only one of the calls made her heart pound— the one that mentioned knowing that Haven had taken Mark to Nordstrom yesterday, and asking what that trip was about. That caller also knew that they had left the department store together, though, it seemed, not where they had gone. But it was way too close for comfort. They were being watched. They were being watched far more intensely than she had imagined.

She cursed herself, her unruly, out-of-control desire for Mark Webster. How had she let this happen, not once, not twice, but three times? How had she allowed herself to be sucked in deeper each time?

She'd chosen sex over her career, that's what she'd done. Like some horny politician Tweeting photos of his dick or accepting blow jobs under the desk.

She had to regain control.

Maybe it was better this way. Rather than waiting for the clock to run out, for Mark to realize she wasn't good enough for him, maybe it was better to be the one who brought things to a neat and tidy conclusion.

"Mark."

He flipped a slice of bacon, and didn't look at her. There must've been something in her voice that warned him he wasn't going to like what she was about to say.

"Someone leaked about the tour. The press is on to us."

"What does that mean?" His tone was suspicious.

"We have to be—we have to be more careful."

"You mean we have to be discreet." He said it flatly. "And I know that really equals 'celibate.'"

"Mark."

"Haven." He crossed his arms to match hers.

"We can't keep doing this."

"Haven. We're not doing 'this.' *This*—" he gestured, encompassing both of them, her apartment, the kitchen, breakfast "—is not a *this*. It's us. It's—"

"It's messy. It's foolish. It's dangerous for you and for your father."

He closed his eyes. "Haven, I like you. I like you way too much for games."

"I know," she said. "I like you way too much for

games, too. That's why we can't play this one. I want you to have what you need, and that means being— *celibate,* if you prefer—for the time being. Until the tour is well underway, or maybe even over."

"Couldn't you drop me as a client? Couldn't I work with someone else?"

"Not now," she said. "Seventeen different reporters know we're working together. If you went to someone else, then everyone would want to know why."

"And we could explain. We could tell the truth."

The truth was evident in how she'd felt with him yesterday. In the dressing room, in the cab, in her bed.

But truth wasn't her job. Jimmy Jeffers had given her a task: clean Mark Webster up, make him ready for the tour. Even if Mark *thought* he didn't want her to, she had to stick with the plan.

And she had to find a way to make him understand.

"Oh, hell," he said, before she could speak. "You don't want to. You want the tour. You'd rather give up what's happening between us for your career, or whatever it represents to you."

"It's not just about *my* career," she said. "It's about *yours*, too, and about your father. I can't turn everything we've both worked for upside down for something that might just be a fantasy. I mean, here we are, and I'm your fairy godmother, right? You know, people write articles about this in image consulting–trade magazines. Don't fall for your creation. It's a huge danger, to make someone over to be exactly who you want them to be, and then when they're how you want them—clean shaven and short-haired and well dressed and behaving like you've told them to, fall in—"

She stopped before the word could pass her lips. His jaw tightened at the omission, and she wondered how he would have reacted if she'd said it out loud, that thing she wasn't sure was true but also wasn't sure wasn't true.

Maybe some people would have had a moment of revelation right then. *Oh, my God, I'm in love with him! Or I might be, anyway!* And they'd stop in their tracks and say, *Love trumps everything, let's throw caution to the wind and just go with the flow here.* But that was only half the equation. Suspecting she might have fallen in love with him didn't tell her anything about how he felt about her. And even if he believed himself to be in love with her—

She cut off her own runaway thoughts. "When you make someone over, you can think they're someone they're not. And they can try too hard to be who you want them to be. That's not good for either of you. You're not my creation, you're a real human being. So let's give you the time to be that person before we complicate things any more."

Mark turned away, then back, his eyes dark. "Don't say, 'let's' like it's a decision I agree to. I hate the idea. What I want is to go back to bed with you and stay there for another few days."

God, that was an appealing suggestion. Her body still held the imprint of his and she craved more, not just of what he could do to her physically, but more of him, the man who knew her weaknesses and wanted her anyway.

But she shook her head slowly. There were vultures closing in on them. "Hiatus," she said. "Mark, *please*."

He hung his head for a moment. Then he straightened and looked her in the eye. "I'll make you a deal. You can have it your way. But first, we eat breakfast. And then we go back to bed."

How much harm could it do? It wouldn't be a hardship to go back to bed with him.

What would be a hardship was stopping after that.

Well, life was tough. Sticking to the plan was difficult. Image was demanding work. But it was good work, too. Necessary work. "And then we take a break."

He nodded. "If that's really what you want."

"It's the right thing for you, too," she said. "Trust me. Going forward, I'll make sure you have an acceptable date on your arm for all the events, and it's not going to be me. I'll find you another date for the fund-raiser. I'll be there, but not with you. Just *there*."

"Making sure I don't screw it up," he said bitterly.

"No—don't be ridiculous. Just—" But of course he was right, wasn't he? She'd be there in case anything went wrong, to rein him in or advise him.

"Will you have a date, too?"

"I think it would be for the best," she said.

"Let the record show, I think this sucks," Mark said.

She nodded. "The record will reflect your feelings."

She wanted to tell him just how much she thought it sucked, too. It caused an ache in the middle of her chest, a lump so big she could barely breathe around it. But she was afraid that he'd talk her out of this if he knew how much she hated it. And right now it felt as if her plan was the only thing keeping her heart safe.

IF HE WAS going to take a forced break—and maybe, though he hoped it wasn't so, a permanent one—from Haven Hoyt, then he was going to make their time together count.

They finished breakfast and cleaned the kitchen, and doing dishes was apparently better foreplay than he'd realized, because when they both reached into the soapy water for the same dish, her fingers had slipped between his, back and forth, in and out, until he lost his mind and crushed her mouth to his in the kind of kiss that went on and on, breaking off only for breath, resuming with more ferocity than before. Their kisses were hungry, and even mean sometimes, and then sweet for as long as they could stand it until they got desperate again.

He stopped only because he wanted to do something else with that mouth of hers. He had ideas and he wanted her to know about them. He wanted to leave her with images in her head and sensations in her body that she wouldn't forget during the weeks or months when they were playing this game of hers.

He didn't believe this was really a game, a hiatus or a break or "let's get these complications off the table" or any of her bullshit. He believed it was an excuse. She couldn't see him in her life or imagine going public with their relationship. In the end, she would choose her image over him because that was what she knew, because that was what was safe for her.

So, screw it, he was going to take every bit of her

that she was offering right now, before she pulled away completely.

"You know earlier?"

"Yes?"

"When you wanted to go down on me and I said *later*?"

She stared at him. Was she holding her breath? Her eyes were wide, and she licked her lips—unconsciously, he thought.

"It's later."

She knelt but he pulled her upright again.

"No. In the bedroom. I want to show you something."

He half herded her into the bedroom, and the look she shot him told him she liked him taking charge as much as he got off on it. He untied her robe and pushed it off her shoulders so it dropped to the floor.

"Lie down. Facedown at the edge of the bed. Right at the edge."

She lay crosswise on the bed, naked, chin close to the side, ass tipped up slightly, which made him want to abandon plan A to climb on top of her and plunge in, instead. But he restrained himself, undoing his jeans but staying put.

"Commando," she observed.

"Yup."

"That's hot." She gazed up at him through thick lashes, which fed some fantasy he hadn't even known he had—her prostrate, helplessly adoring.

Man, maybe he was as much of an asshole as the world thought. "My image consultant wouldn't approve." He took himself in hand and made a show of it, a slow, sensuous slide up and down his length, his thumb smoothing a drop of pre-cum over the head.

"Your image consultant could not approve more."

"My image consultant needs to convey her approval, then." He shed his jeans and came close, so his thighs pressed against the edge of the bed.

He had all manner of images in mind, but what she did surprised him completely. Which was to say, it was unlike the Haven he'd thought he'd known and so much like the Haven he seemed to have invoked from sheer desire. She rubbed her nose into the fold of his thigh, scenting him. "You smell so good," she said.

"*That's* hot," he said.

In answer, she licked him. His thigh, then his balls, then the length of his cock, which jerked its endorsement. She caught his head between her lips and popped it out again, sending a shock of pleasure he felt all the way to the root and as far off as his skull. She did it again, and then she took him deep. He felt the hot, wet satin of the back of her throat, firm against his sensitive tip. She pressed him deeper.

"Jesus."

There was the physical pleasure itself, which was massive, heat and slide and pressure and pull, the suction as her cheeks hollowed, the play of her tongue along his length and under the ridge of his head. And then there was the rest of it, the fact that she was letting him so deep, that she wasn't guarding herself against him with her hands or restricting his movement, just trusting him not to hurt her.

She slid her palm under his balls, the other around to his ass, urging him deeper still.

"You sure?"

In answer, she hummed in her throat.

Holy *hell*.

He was so deep in her mouth that her lips reached almost to his base. He was torn between wanting this to last forever and the primal need to come as soon as possible. He imagined the spasms of her throat and the spasms of his cock, and almost spilled right then.

She made contented noises as she withdrew and slid down again, her lips loosening and tightening, her hands massaging his thighs, moving him closer, pushing him farther away. He wanted to do something for her, too, so he stroked a hand along her back, reaching to touch her smooth, round cheeks. She lifted her ass into his hand, tipping back until his fingers, almost of their own accord, slid down and into her, into heat and wet and—

"You're getting off on sucking me."

She answered by curling her tongue again around the head of his cock and dropping her hand down to apply pressure to his taint. She was on her elbows and her knees, now, dipping her head, her pelvis tilted to present as much of herself as possible to his hand.

"You like it. You're not just doing it to be nice."

He twisted his fingers inside her, and she bucked back against his hand, seeking more, groaning around his erection.

"What if I mess with your nipple with this hand, and

then put my thumb inside you and then crook my fingers around and—"

In answer, she came, whimpering against his cock, spasming around his fingers. He immediately urged her onto her back, and knelt on the bed over her. Quickly he found a condom in the night-table drawer, and before her aftershocks were finished, he was in her, taking her through the last of the pulses, his own orgasm shooting up from the soles of his feet and gripping him until it shook him limp.

Haven.

"I think you had it all wrong," he said. "You don't like it neat. You like it messy. You like it hard and dirty and—"

"I think…" she said uncertainly. Her breath was warm on his shoulder. "I think I like—*you.*"

11

PETE SOVEREIGN HAD relocated their coffee date from a big, busy Starbucks to a coffee shop that he'd described as "intimate and cozy," and when she showed up, he was sitting at a table near the door with two mugs and two plates in front of him. He pushed one of each across the table to her. "Let me guess," he said. "Decaf mocha with skim and a warm chocolate croissant."

Actually, what she usually ordered was a double espresso straight up and a crispy rice treat, but she thanked him and sat. She'd never been pulled over for drunk driving, but right now she felt as though she was walking heel-to-toe along the yellow divider, pacing out the narrow line between yielding to Pete's whims and telling him to go to hell. Somehow everything depended on her slightly impaired ability to balance, for her sake and for Mark's. Pete held both of their careers hostage, and she couldn't just blow him off.

But *God* she wanted to tell him to take a hike.

He gave her a complete once-over, staring down her

shirt. Then he said, "So. Have you had enough of Mark Webster yet?"

There was that attitude again. She knew he wanted her to smile conspiratorially; to say, "Mark's great!" with her voice and, "We both know better!" with her eyes.

She hadn't had enough of Mark Webster, though, and she wasn't quite sure she'd ever have enough. She wasn't sure she even knew what it would mean for her to have enough of Mark Webster, and the mere thought sent a reverberation of pleasure through her.

This will be over in half an hour and you will avoid Pete Sovereign like the plague after that, she told herself.

"Mark and I get along well," she said. "I'm sorry to hear you and he didn't." And then she thought that maybe her response had been the worst of both worlds—not the sly agreement Pete had been trying to coax out of her, and not enough of an endorsement of Mark's strengths.

"It wasn't that I didn't get along with him," said Pete breezily. "He didn't get along with me."

"Well, whichever it was, I hope you can see that doing this tour is in *both* of your best interests."

"Is it?"

"There's a lot of money and exposure in it for you."

"What else is in it for me?" Pete asked, and there was no missing the note of invitation.

She'd expected this. Once Mark had told her what had happened between him and Pete, she'd understood their past vividly. There were many things she couldn't know—how much of Pete's interest in Lyn had been in Lyn herself, how much had been straight-across sexual envy of Mark, and how much had been fed by ambition. But it was clear that the seeds of rivalry were deeply sown, and it was just as clear that Pete was determined to find a way to use her to get to Mark.

She had to divert him, had to redirect his jealousy or lust or whatever it was. If she could somehow play straight to his weaknesses, his vanity and his ego, she might have a shot.

And then she saw her angle. "What's in it for you? The chance to work on your public image."

"My image?"

She'd surprised him, set him back on his heels, and she savored the victory. "When was the last time you looked yourself up online? Have you searched for yourself to see what people are saying about you on Twitter?"

He'd recovered his bluster. "I don't need to ego surf to know where I stand."

"There are very few people in the world who wouldn't benefit from some image improvement consulting."

"Are you saying there's something wrong with my image?"

"I'm just saying that I think you and I can make a deal."

She saw his eyes flick back to her cleavage, and she added, "A purely business deal."

"So few things in the world are pure," he murmured.

"Business," she repeated firmly.

Something flared behind his eyes, but he nodded. "State your terms."

"If you drop whatever your vendetta is against Mark and agree to do the tour, I'll throw in a bunch of free image advice as we go along. I can give you tips and pointers. We're talking hundreds, if not thousands, of dollars of insight. But you have to stop holding the tour over Mark's head."

"Does Mark know you're making this deal?"

"Yes," she lied.

She hadn't told Mark she was having coffee with Pete because she knew how much he didn't want her to. And she *definitely* hadn't told him she was cutting a deal with Pete because she was pretty sure Mark would be livid with rage.

"Why is it so important to you to give him such a hard time, anyway?" she asked.

He wouldn't meet her gaze.

Something in his expression knocked a puzzle piece into place for her, and all at once, she knew. "You were in love with Lyn before she started sleeping with Mark."

"That's bullshit." He pushed his chair away from the table and stood up, his jaw hard and his shoulders high. "Fuck this. Forget it. I don't need to make a deal with you or anyone else. I don't need Mark Webster's crap, or yours."

She had almost blown it. She'd slipped, lost track. Seeing that Pete had been hurt by what happened between him and Mark had made her soften toward him and play the hand badly.

But Pete wasn't anywhere near ready to admit to her

that he'd lost something in the scuffle over Lyn, and she couldn't afford to have him walk out on her now. Mark couldn't afford it.

"Wait!"

Pete hesitated.

"Come back. Forget I said that. Look. What do we need to do to convince you?"

He stood there, arms crossed, expression dark. Then a slight smile turned up the corners of his mouth, and that was way scarier than the darkness. "I heard Mark's speaking at the Noteworthy fund-raiser."

Uh-oh.

"I want to give that speech."

"Do you really care about kids and music lessons?" she asked.

"Nope, but neither does Mark."

"He does," she said, but she knew it was futile to try to argue this with Pete.

"The point of that speech isn't that I give a crap about kids' music lessons. It's that it'll be good publicity and it'll make me look good. It'll be good for my *image*, right?" His tone mocked her.

Haven sighed. "I can't give you that," she said. "The programs are printed, the PR firm has already gotten the word out."

"Are you gonna be there?"

"Yes."

"With Mark?"

"Mark's going to be there with Cindy Sheldon." Cindy was a classically trained singer with widespread popular appeal, the type who had her own Christmas and children's lullaby albums. Cindy had the perfect image to help rehab Mark's—she was beautiful, refined, heavily involved in charitable work and musical in a clean, unblemished way. And Cindy, by being seen with Mark, would reach out to a wider audience of pop lovers, increase her pop-music street cred.

"Go with me," Pete said.

For a moment she didn't understand.

"Be my date," he clarified.

Oh, *God.*

Of all the—

And yet she wasn't really surprised, because she'd known this was Pete's endgame. He wanted to stick it to Mark in a way that would hurt, the way it had hurt Pete—still hurt Pete, apparently—that Mark had slept with Lyn.

"That's not a good idea."

"Why not?"

Because you and Mark have a history. Because I can't be the second woman to be "shared" between you guys. Because it would kill Mark, and that would kill me.

Only she couldn't say that. They'd made it this far without Pete getting wind of the fact that she and Mark were…what they were.

"Look," Pete said. "I need a date to the fund-raiser. And you need me to agree to do this tour. It's a mutually beneficial deal. And to return to your earlier point, if it makes you feel better, I promise I won't try anything."

She couldn't. Even if she was dying to strike a bargain with Pete to save the tour and get him off their backs, she couldn't. Now that she'd heard Mark's story, there was no way she could put him through that again. All he would see was Pete triumphing. Pete *getting the girl*. Pete looking like the winner in the media.

"I'm sorry," she said. "I can't. Anything but that. It would be a media fiasco that would jeopardize the tour."

He crossed his arms, scrunched his brow. "Why do you care so much, huh? What does it matter to you whether this tour happens or not?"

"I told Jimmy Jeffers I'd get Mark Webster ready to tour. If there's no tour, there's no job."

But that wasn't the truth anymore. In reality, what she cared about now was how Mark looked when he talked about his father, his wonder at being given a second chance at father–son bonding. She cared about the abandon on Mark's face when he played music, his thoughtfulness when he taught guitar. And—

His intensity *when he looked at her*.

"—thing I don't understand is why Mark cares so much," Pete was saying. "He never gave a shit about the band. It was always beneath him. He was a *musician*."

"He's got his reasons," she said. "And so do you. So, yeah, think about it. And do what's best for you *and* for your career. Okay?"

He made a disgusted face and turned from her to stare at the window.

She got up, threw away her trash and headed for the door.

What a mess. Pete still hadn't agreed to do the tour, and now he'd talked himself into a fund-raiser all three of them would have to attend on Saturday, along with a good portion of New York's music journalists.

Danger. Ragged edges. Pianos suspended overhead from wires. Dominoes cued to fall.

And most of all, the look on Mark's face when he found out she'd met with Pete behind his back.

MARK WAS TRYING desperately not to be a douche. He was attempting to give his undivided attention to the very tall, very thin, very charming woman next to him, rather than craning his neck to see if Haven had arrived at the Noteworthy fund-raiser—and who she was with.

He was supposed to be escorting, and be *seen* with, pop sensation Cindy Sheldon. Except, of course, he wanted to *see* Haven.

"This is lovely," said Cindy, in her smooth, gorgeous alto.

"It is," he said, because she was a nice woman, well-meaning, and the alternative was to tell her what he was really thinking. He hated these things. *Hated them.* It was even worse tonight because he was expected to "say a few words." His stage fright had overshadowed his excitement about helping with such a great cause. It was like a hand around his throat right now.

The event was black-and-white themed—"with a splash of color," according to the invitation. The dress code made it practically impossible to pick anyone out of the crowd, let alone a petite woman in what he—with a throb of anticipation—knew would be a teeny-tiny black dress.

The ballroom was decked out in elaborate, expensive,

black-and-white decorations—potted trees wrapped in silver and hung with black-and-white baubles, garlands of black-and-white fabric draped everywhere. The band played a lively tune and lines had formed at the open bar.

This was his own personal hell, reminding him of why he hated to perform at weddings. He felt awkward and self-conscious, like a boy playing dress-up. His tux strained across his shoulders, even though it was the size he always rented. Too much lifting, maybe—to take his mind off his sexual frustration, he'd been hitting the gym harder than usual.

Surreptitiously, he scanned the room for Haven again. He didn't want to hurt Cindy's feelings but he had to know where Haven was.

"Ooh!" cried Cindy. Hors d'oeuvres on a silver platter had materialized in front of them, courtesy of a smiling waitress, and he took a small mushroom puff while Cindy loaded up her napkin-covered palm. Not his kind of food, really. Too schmoofy. He bit into the puff (were you supposed to eat it all in one bite or not? He couldn't remember, if he'd ever known). Bits of flaky crust floated down and landed all over his tux jacket, like a really bad case of dandruff. He tried to brush it off and left a little grease smear. Great.

He spotted Haven then. How could he have doubted that he'd find her? He'd know her anywhere, an impression of her size and shape, and the energy contained in her compact body as identifiable and unique as a fingerprint. She was, as he'd predicted, wearing a little black dress, but his imagination had been inadequate. The dress bared her back, a smooth expanse of skin he wanted to rest his palm against. When she turned, desire stabbed him in the chest. The dress had skinny little straps and a deep scoop neckline that skimmed along breasts he'd felt against his lips and tongue— that he could *still* feel against his lips and tongue. His fingers flexed slightly at the thought as he relived the sensation of her body clenching around him. *Jesus*. She should *not* have worn that dress. Not if she was serious about what she'd said to him about taking a hiatus. What about this was *discreet*?

Of course she was serious. Haven Hoyt was serious about everything.

For reasons known only to God, that set off a series of flashbulb images for him. The way she'd kissed him in her office, the way she'd felt against his tongue, coming in the dressing room, the way she'd looked on all fours on her bed, his cock disappearing between her red lips, her ass tipped up to find his hand.

The tux pants were *not* going to cut him any slack if he didn't shut down this trip down memory lane ASAP.

Cindy moaned with hors d'oeuvres–induced ecstasy, but he barely registered it, other than to be grateful she was distracted by food so he could stare at Haven. Haven had told him, via text, that she'd warned Cindy he wasn't interested in anything other than friendship and some see-and-be-seen dating.

Staking your claim? he'd texted back.

Trying to simplify your life a little.

Keeping his hands off Haven, exercising "discretion," had been *killing* him, absolutely destroying him. The two of them had to be in close proximity frequently because they were working together to preparc Mark for tonight's speech and for the exclusive interview that Haven had decided to grant Suellen Marvel at *High Note*. Most of the time they worked in Haven's office. The office itself, and the fact that she always kept the door open, were like taunts to Mark. *Remember what you did against this door, less than a week ago? You're not doing it right now.*

Haven had not prohibited Mark from bringing up or discussing sex, so he did it as frequently as he thought he could get away with. Which was pretty much all the time. That meant he couldn't get it off his mind, either. While he was trying to make her lose control, while he was indulging his fantasy that he would say just the right thing to convince her that she needed to go shut that door right now, he was also making himself rock hard and totally frustrated.

Once he'd lowered his voice to a whisper, leaned in, and said, "I was just thinking about the way you looked spread out for me on your bed."

She'd rolled her eyes, but the fierce blush that rose in her cheeks gave her away. "We're not doing this, Mark."

She'd probably said that to him a hundred times since the night and morning they'd spent at her place. One of his only sources of consolation was that she sounded less and less sure each time she said it.

She was not very good at hiding how she felt, which was the only thing that made this period of celibacy bearable. That and sexting.

Okay, it wasn't exactly sexting. It was texting that slipped over the line into flirting and then, just once or twice, over the line into something that didn't quite entirely count as celibacy. Those texts required him to perform marvelous feats of coordination, during which he used his right hand for the purpose for which God had so deftly crafted it, and his left hand to keep the conversation going.

Haven had apparently not been able to stop herself from engaging with him via text. She'd said one or two things in texts that he couldn't imagine her saying in real life, things about body parts of his that she particularly liked, and where she would like him to put them, preferably as soon as possible. Afterward, after she sent him a lot of nonsense characters to indicate the heights to which sexting had taken her, she also denied that it counted as sex and exhorted him, once again, to be discreet. (Exact words: "Don't you dare lose your phone.")

But what she hadn't said was where this was all going, and that was the part that was killing him.

And speaking of killing him, a man had just materialized at Haven's side. A tall, dark, handsome man who looked completely at ease in their posh surroundings. The bastard was laughing and taking Haven's arm and making small talk and—God*dammit*—feeding Haven an hors d'oeuvre.

Mark went hot with jealousy at the sight of that man's fingers in Haven's mouth. Jealousy and totally inappropriate lust, because he'd been in Haven's mouth in every way it was possible to be there, and if that guy didn't keep his hands to himself, in about thirty seconds

Mark would cross the room, wrench her out of the man's grasp and kiss the hell out of her in front of everyone.

Ironically, Cindy chose that moment to feed *him*, her slim fingers lingering a tiny bit too long on his lips and tongue. He chewed and swallowed and said, "I don't want you to get the wrong idea, Cindy."

"Haven told me we're just having fun. But no point in not having all the fun we can, right?"

"Look," he said. "I *really* appreciate your helping me out with this. But I'm actually not even in the market for fun right now."

Which was crazy. When hadn't he been in the market for fun? And why was he refusing an offer like this out of loyalty to a woman who had put him on a hiatus of an indeterminate duration and, when he thought of it, an indeterminate nature, too?

"Mark," said a female voice at his elbow. He jumped, but it wasn't Haven. It was Becca Steele, who did PR for Noteworthy. "They're ready for you on stage."

He thought he was going to throw up.

"You'll be great," said Cindy, smiling.

He followed Becca into the wings and waited his turn. By the time he got out on stage, people had sat at the dinner tables, and servers were bringing around salads. His stomach coiled at the sight of food, and then twice as hard at the sight of all those faces staring up at him.

"I'm thrilled to introduce Mark Webster, formerly of the band Sliding Up," Becca told the rapt audience. "You probably remember 'Twice as Nice'?"

The crowd murmured its approval.

"Mark's here to talk to us a little bit about how music lessons changed his life."

When she stepped back, he stood for a moment with the mic in his hand. He wasn't sure he could even speak. And then he found Haven in the crowd, and she smiled at him. A full-on smile of pride and delight, and he thought, *I can do this*.

"I'm better with playing guitar than speaking," he said. His voice was huge and echoey in the ballroom, but it sounded okay. Steady. "But I was told you wouldn't appreciate me singing my speech."

Laughter.

"It takes a lot to make me talk in public. I was never the guy in the band who did the witty little interludes."

More laughter.

"So you know if I'm up here talking to you, it's because it's about something really important."

They were watching and listening, and to his shock, he was enjoying this. They were waiting for him to say something, and he had something to say.

"My dad, who raised me pretty much on his own, was a good guy. He wanted the best for me. But there wasn't much for me at school."

He told them how he hadn't been particularly good at academics. Or at sitting still. He'd been just getting by, he said, and slipping back as the work got harder and there were more and more kids who were just plain smarter than he was. He'd been a wisp of a kid back then, and he had friends, but only a few. He had been shy and quiet and not particularly athletic at that point.

"Now you wouldn't want to meet me on the basketball court," he said, grinning, and they laughed again.

That laughter was as much of a high as the applause had once been. Better, because he was doing something that came straight from his soul. This laughter felt like the applause he got for playing the blues, or the smile on Gavin's face when Mark had shown him that guitar lick.

"And then one of the older kids in the neighborhood handed me something. It could have been a bong or my first beer or a crack pipe or a cigarette, but it wasn't. It was a guitar. He let me play his guitar. And everything changed for me. Practically overnight."

A deep hush descended, one he could feel in his own body.

"I started doing better in school because my dad and teachers told me I could only have guitar lessons if I kept up my grades. And suddenly I had friends, because a guy with a guitar was cool and useful. A guy with a guitar got the girls."

More laughter.

"I've had my tough moments," he said.

The faces in the audience were upturned. He saw sympathy, not judgment for what he'd done wrong. These people were hearing his story, and they were seeing him as a human being.

"But music has always been the thing that saved me. I believe music can be that thing for a lot of kids. The way many kids are saved by sports or by learning to write about their experiences. And those kids who are saved that way—they go on to do important things. They change culture and history and politics. They make our world a better place."

His blood thrummed with it, that feeling. He was doing something that mattered. He was telling the truth. His truth.

"Bid high," he said. "Bid frequently. For the kid I was. For all our kids."

The applause was thunderous. He shook hands with Becca and began his descent from the stage. He saw Cindy first, coming toward him to congratulate him.

Right behind her was Haven, beaming at him as she crossed the floor, date in tow.

All the joy drained out of the moment. Oh, God, he was going to have to meet Mr. Whoever and make nice talk. All the while knowing—

Knowing what? What did he know, *really*? Haven had told him she would bring a date to this, hadn't she? What claim did Mark have on her? Haven had had sex with him, had enjoyed herself in ways that were unusual for her. But he didn't know why or what it meant to her or whether she wanted anything more to ever happen between them.

Even though he did.

He wanted to be more to Haven than a novelty, more than a plaything, more, even, than part of her journey of sexual self-discovery.

He wanted Haven in his life, because Haven had made so much in his life feel right, and real.

She was getting closer, and there was so very, very little to her dress, so much bare, smooth, curvy Haven. His hands were twitchy with the need to touch her, and his mouth was watering. His heart felt tight with the need to tell her what she meant to him.

Her date placed a proprietary hand against the center of Haven's bare back and Mark felt something deep and ill-defined snap inside him.

"Mark, that was brilli—"

He didn't give her a chance to finish, didn't let her introduce the man with the wandering hand. He just grabbed her arm and murmured, gruffly, "I need to talk to you."

She looked startled for a split second. Then she gently removed her arm from his grasp and smoothed her expression out, bringing her polished social self to the rescue. "Well, hello to you, too," she said sweetly, ignoring the urgency in his low whisper. "Don Dormer, this is Mark Webster and Cindy Sheldon…"

Haven continued her suave introductions—Cindy would of course be familiar to Don as the singer on that *amazing* Christmas album that was so popular last year, Don was the president of an up-and-coming sports cable station…

"Great speech. Really great speech," said Don, putting out his hand. His shake was firm. He looked Mark in the eye. There was nothing anywhere in his demeanor to indicate anything other than the greatest ease and comfort in this situation, and Mark imagined you could drop this guy anywhere and he'd be exactly the same. Totally in control, totally on top of the world. Mark hadn't been privy to Haven's conversation with Elisa when she arranged this date, but he could imagine it. *Yes, someone who fits in perfectly at a fund-raiser. The kind of guy you don't have to watch out for or worry about whether he'll do something embarrassing...*

Mark didn't want Haven anywhere near this guy. Or any other guy. Not for the duration of the tour. Not for a few months, a few weeks, a few days, or the few hours it would take before this fund-raiser ended and they could all go home. He wanted her to be his right now, and his alone.

"Hav—I need to talk to you." He said it more gently this time. It came out sounding a lot more civilized than he felt, but still pretty harsh.

"If you'd excuse me? Mark and I have been working hard preparing for a media exclusive with *High Note*, and we've had an awful game of phone tag today. We'll just be a couple of minutes trying to sort a few critical things out."

"Sure thing," said Don, and turned to Cindy.

"This had better be good," Haven said, as she followed Mark. "We're supposed to be inconspicuous."

"I remember. Discreet." He led her out of the ballroom, around the corner, and up a half flight of carpeted stairs to a small mezzanine area. The spot was relatively quiet and afforded at least some privacy. Also, it was about twenty-five degrees cooler here than it had been in the ballroom.

"Are you okay?" she asked, concern wrinkling her forehead.

"It was hot in there."

"I wasn't hot."

"You aren't wearing any clothes."

She crossed her arms and glared at him. "This is

awkward, Mark. We're not supposed to be sneaking off together, leaving our dates to fend for themselves. The whole point of this is to divert any possible suspicion away from us."

"No," said Mark, taking a step toward her. She retreated, and he chased her back till her shoulder blades pressed against the wall behind her, an echo of that first time against her office door. She gasped, an innocent sound that nevertheless wrapped itself around his cock and tugged.

"No," he said again, and he kissed her. Not a tentative, exploratory kiss, but a kiss into which he could pour the depth of his feelings. *You are mine, and I'm telling, not asking.*

For a moment she struggled. Then she gave in, and when she did, she did it completely. Molded herself against him, the length of her body easing against the length of his. She slid her hands around the back of his neck and wove her fingers into his hair as she slid her tongue along his. She opened up to him and leaned in.

It made him want to cry with relief.

12

HE PULLED BACK, held her face between his hands, and told her, "*That's* the whole point. The whole point is that I like you *way* too much to pretend to you or myself or the world that you mean nothing to me."

She was so startled by the kiss, by her own out-of-control lust, that it took a while for his words to sink in. At last she understood that he was telling her something big. Something real. Mark Webster was asking her for something that she *knew* he hadn't been able to ask of anyone since Lyn had broken his heart.

And not only that—the thing he wanted from her was something she wanted just as much.

That was the surprise. Her belly warmed and her heart opened up. Her whole body along with her mind reached out to him, all ready to say, *Yes, yes, I want that, too.*

She'd loved his speech. Loved the way he'd gotten up there looking so ill at ease, as if he was wearing not only an outfit but also a role that felt wrong, and then…

then, when he'd put his hand on the microphone, he'd changed in an instant. An expression, a whole new way of standing, had come over him as if he commanded not only the device in his hand but also by extension the whole room. All of them fell under his spell, the way an audience did when he played. And then he gave his speech, and it was like hearing him play. She *felt* him. That had been Mark to his core, to his soul, to that part of him she was most envious of, that part she was still not sure she possessed.

She was proud of him. She wanted to belong to him.

Maybe this wasn't so difficult after all. Maybe it was the simplest thing in the world. Maybe she could follow her heart and figure out the rest as they went along.

She'd done that once before and it had ended badly, but that didn't mean it had to end badly all the time. Screw Cinderella and Pygmalion and Eliza Doolittle. Mark was here tonight. He was a little rough around the edges, maybe, but that was part of his appeal. Maybe he could live in her world when he needed to, and she could live in his.

"Okay," she said.

"Okay?" He sounded startled.

"Yeah. We can make that happen." She leaned in close and touched her mouth to his, sweeping her tongue across his upper lip. He opened to her, his mouth relaxing against hers.

"Huh," said a voice. "You got the bonus package— image consulting *and* tongue."

Pete Sovereign.

Of course.

"Can't fault your taste," Pete said to Mark. "She's hot."

She could feel the energy gathering in Mark, and she grasped desperately for something she could say to defuse the situation. Something she could say that would keep this from going any further awry.

"Hav?" a voice called.

It was Suellen Marvel from *High Note*, cresting the stairs to the mezzanine. And behind her, Becca Steele, the marketing director of Noteworthy. She guessed they'd come to see if they could get Mark to talk about the speech.

The appearance of the women was a reprieve, possibly salvation, in fact. They presented the perfect way to rescue the situation and get Pete's and Mark's minds off their hatred of each other. Sure, there would still be a lot of work to do to defuse the tension, but at least things hadn't exploded, as she'd thought for a moment was inevitable. She grasped Mark's arm firmly, intending to lead him toward Suellen and Becca, and far away from Pete Sovereign.

Pete crossed his arms. He wasn't trying to hide his cockiness from her now, the way he had that day in her office. The gloves were off. "Did Haven tell you I asked her to come to this thing with me tonight?" he said to Mark. "We had a *great* coffee date last week, and it seemed like a natural fit."

Mark's eyes found hers.

She wordlessly pleaded with him. *It's not what you think. Trust me enough to believe that.* But all that came out of her mouth was, "He asked but I said no."

Mark's gaze wouldn't hold hers. It sought Pete again, and he took a step forward. She tugged his arm, but he didn't budge. "Mark," she whispered.

Suellen's eyes followed the action, flicking rapidly from one of them to the other. She had the avid look that reporters got when a situation blew up. Thrill of the chase.

"She did say no," Pete confirmed. "And now I know why. She was plenty busy, what with having a date to the fund-raiser already, and having you on the side. But no worries," he said to Haven. "Take your time. And when you're done with Mark, I'll take over. That's the way it works, you know. Mark first, and then when you're ready for a real musician—"

Out of the corner of her eye, she saw Mark lunge.

"No," she cried.

It was too late. Mark's hands connected with Pete's throat. A crowd gathered—where had these people come from?—and several men grabbed both Mark and Pete, hauling them off each other. Mark flailed wildly, trying to escape his captors, his face twisted in rage.

Cell phones came out, held aloft for photos and video, and Haven watched it all, her thoughts a tangle at the wreckage of her work all around her.

All these people were seeing firsthand what it was like for her world to fall apart.

"Are they fighting over you?"

Trust Suellen to ask that question. The journalist's tone recalled her to herself, like a slap in the face. This was her job. This was what she did. She answered tough questions. She cleaned up messes. No way would she lose control here. For Mark's career and for her own, she would hold the pieces together.

"You know these guys have a long history. Lots of old tensions," Haven said, and was proud of how cool she sounded. How unconcerned. As if her clients got in brawls all the time and it was just part of the long image-rehab process. As if it had absolutely nothing to do with her.

"Are you and Mark Webster together?"

"We'll talk about all of this during the exclusive." She took a deep breath. She could fix this. This is what she did. She could spin it. She could talk about how she and Mark were attracted to each other—"Who could resist such a hot guitarist?" she'd laugh—but had decided that dating wasn't compatible with working together, so they'd put it off. That sounded fine. And then she'd say how Pete had a lot of envy issues with Mark, and had gotten the wrong idea.

She'd tell the world what had really happened between Pete and Mark when the band had broken up. This wasn't a disaster. It was an opportunity.

And then she saw Mark's face.

Dark. His expression, savage, aimed not at Pete but at *her.*

Regret choked her. And panic. She knew instantly that she'd been focused on the wrong priority. This wasn't about fixing things with the public. What mattered was Mark. Her and Mark.

She knew what she needed to do, if she wanted him to ever look at her again the way he had in Nordstrom's and in her apartment. She needed to answer Suellen's question with the simple truth. *Yes, we're together.*

Her mind raced through all her years of training, scanning the situation, looking for words, trying to foresee consequences. There would be so much sorting out for her to do, so much for Mark to do. They would lose things that mattered. She could do that, but for Mark—

Pete still hadn't committed to the tour. Her handling of this moment would dictate how this scene played out in the press—and whether Pete saw the tour as a train wreck or his ticket to easy money. It could make or break Mark's role, too—if Jimmy Jeffers decided that she and Mark were too much of a liability as a couple, he could trot that replacement out again.

Her next words might very well determine whether or not Mark would be able to take care of his father.

Could she make that decision for him?

She tried to catch his eye, to ask him without words—*What do you want me to do?*

He wouldn't engage. That fury was written so deep on his face, and his eyes darted away from hers.

"Dammit, Hav," Mark said, his words hard, bitten off. "She asked if we're together. It's not a really hard question."

Suellen had apparently given up on Haven. "Are you guys together?" the reporter was asking Mark.

"We were," he said.

Then he walked away.

W*E WERE.*

If it had never really been a relationship, officially, did it count as a breakup?

It felt like a breakup. The coldness of his eyes, the hard set of his jaw. The accusation in his expression.

That one word, that little *were*, had hit her like a sucker punch. It was the force, the pain, of realizing that something important—no, something essential, as essential as breath or the beating of her own heart—was gone. She had hesitated, she hadn't seen what mattered fast enough. She hadn't stood up for the person, the relationship, that mattered most to her in the world. How could she blame him, when she'd already eroded his faith in her so much that he hadn't believed she could make any other choice?

He'd walked away.

Of course he'd walked away.

She would have done exactly the same thing.

She turned her back on Suellen, on the crowd. She'd never done that before. Out the door of the hotel and down the street she ran, catching up to Mark as he tried to flag down a cab.

There wasn't a cab to be seen, fortunately. In a city full of cabs, when you were trying to flee, you were almost guaranteed not to be able to hail one. In this case it worked in her favor.

"Mark."

"Don't bother." His voice was icy, his posture rigid.

"I'm sorry. I—" She couldn't figure out the right words. Everything she could possibly say seemed so painfully inadequate. "I should have—"

"You know what? I'm glad I know the truth. You're ashamed of me. Better to know now than later."

That caught her off guard. "I'm not *ashamed* of you, Mark. I was going to tell her the truth."

"When? How long was it going to take you? How

many other excuses and lies were going to come out of your mouth first?"

The sick hurt swerved and became a little spark of anger. "I was trying to help you! I didn't want everything you'd worked for to blow up in your face."

"Oh, really? Because that's sure as hell not what it looked like. Look closely at yourself, Haven. Tell *me* the truth at least. Can you picture a scenario where you put your arm around me, rest your head on my shoulder, and say, 'This is my boyfriend, Mark Webster? Burnout, has-been, drunk, brawler, scruffy unshaven guy with shit taste in clothes.' Me." He left the edge of the curb and paced as he spat out the words, his brisk, angry steps taking him close enough for her to reach out and touch his sleeve—if she'd wanted to, if he hadn't been bristling with frustration and self-loathing.

Every word he said pierced her, each one of those angry, self-abusing descriptors. Suddenly she realized how he saw himself, and by extension how he thought she saw him. How could he still believe that? How could he think that about her, about *himself* after what they had been through together? "God, Mark. Any other way you can tear yourself down? Because, man, you really do make that sound appealing."

"But that's who I am, Haven. You don't want the real me. The real me disgusts you. I think you might be more right than I wanted to admit that you only want me if I can be your—what was the example you used? Frankenstein's monster?"

"Pygmalion," she said.

He pointed an accusing finger at her. "You only want

me if you can trot me out in public and I fit in just perfectly and the time is right and nothing is out of place."

It hit home, and yet she heard, under the all-too-accurate words, *his* terror. "Is that what you're afraid of?"

"Don't make this about me. Don't fucking make this about me and *my* fear. I'm not the only one who let all that public sex happen. You wanted to get caught. You've got all this stuff inside you that you keep hidden. You want people to know you but you won't let anyone in, and if someone gets close enough to figure out who you really are, then you—"

She watched, saw the moment the anger drained out of his face to be replaced with the hurt she'd seen in the ballroom.

"Then you push him away."

She wanted to deny it, but there was too much in her head, too much in her heart. It had hurt him when he thought she was going to lie about their relationship in there, and she didn't know how to undo her failure to claim him. How could she make it right? How could she take back pushing him away so she could make him believe she meant it?

She had lied by omission because when push had come to shove, that's what her instinct told her to do. She had denied him by failing to claim him when it really mattered. This was exactly what she'd told Elisa she feared.

What the hell did she *really* want?

Mark held a hand up, and she saw an empty cab coming up the street.

He stepped to the curb and opened the door. "I don't know what you're scared of, but— Look, I want to be with you, but not like this. Not until you're ready, until you know what you want."

And he stepped back and held the door wide for her.

"Mark," she began. But she didn't know what she wanted or how to say it. She didn't know how to not be scared and just tell him all the things she felt.

"Go," he said.

"I—"

"Go, or I will."

"Lady," said the cab driver. "Get in the goddamned cab already. I don't have all night."

"Mark," she tried again, but he was already gone, his shoulders hunched as he headed up the street away from her.

13

"WHAT ARE YOU DOING?"

"Eating Cheetos," Haven said, shoving another big handful into her mouth.

Elisa tilted her head to one side.

"What?" Haven demanded.

"I've never seen you eat Cheetos like that."

"I've never had my career and my sex life implode simultaneously in public before."

"Do you want another Water Lily?" Elisa got up from the couch and crossed to the kitchen area of Haven's apartment, where the ingredients for the cocktails were arrayed on the counter.

"Yes. Can you make the next one stronger?"

"It's all alcohol, baby. You just have to drink them faster. Or stop eating Cheetos so they absorb faster."

"Can't," said Haven.

Elisa paused in the midst of squeezing a lemon and arched a brow. "Hav? Are you in love with him?"

It was a question Haven had been desperately trying

not to ask herself. She'd been drowning even the hint of that question in work, dealing with administrative issues that under other circumstances she would have happily procrastinated for years. Methodically calling, emailing and texting back reporters to tell them she was sorry but she had promised *High Note* an exclusive. Trying to figure out how, exactly, she was going to explain the events of Saturday night to Suellen. In short, she was doing anything to avoid the question that Elisa now posed.

"No," said Haven.

Elisa set the lemon down and reached for the crème de violette. "Are you *sure* about that?"

"Positive. It was just really good sex."

"I think you're going to need to tell me a little bit about this really good sex."

"I don't want to talk about it."

"About the sex?"

"About any of it."

After Mark had walked up the street last night, Haven had gotten out of the cab (much to the driver's fury) and gone back into the fund-raiser. She had no choice, because nothing screamed scandal louder than running away. Reporters swarmed her when she returned, and she made herself smile at them like nothing was wrong. She pretended that she understood what had just happened to her and she'd planned it all to go this way.

"Do you know the history between Pete Sovereign and Mark Webster?" a reporter demanded.

"Let's keep the focus on the kids," Haven said. "Pete Sovereign and Mark Webster came here tonight to give children access to musical instruments. Whatever history is between them, they thought these kids were more important."

"What's going on between you and Mark Webster?"

"Anything you need to know about my *working* relationship with Mark Webster will be in the exclusive I've granted to Suellen Marvel at *High Note*."

"Is it just a working relationship?"

"I'll remind you again that we're here for the kids," Haven had said firmly. Coolly. Even if she'd been nowhere near cool inside. More like suffering from alternating flashes of hot shame and ice-cold fear.

"Did you know Pete just made a public statement that he's agreed to do the tour? Says he pities Mark because there's nothing worse than a public breakup. Says that's enough humiliation for one week."

She wasn't surprised. Trust Pete to find a way to add another layer to Mark's defeat.

She'd stayed until the end of the fund-raiser, then taken a cab home. She kicked her shoes off, stripped out of her dress, let down her hair, and went to bed with her makeup on. In the morning her pillow would be gritty and black with mascara, but she didn't give a crap.

She'd been numb at first, but as she started to warm up, as her body relaxed into sleep, she'd begun to cry. Tears flowed for the work she'd done to become the best of the best—all the clients she'd wooed, the image she'd made for herself, and all the people whose public personae were tied up with hers.

She refused to shed a tear for Mark Webster and the way he'd kissed her and claimed her on the mezzanine.

Not for what he'd made her want, how he'd made her forget herself and all the boundaries that kept her life neat and clean. And above all, not for the way he made her feel. Alive. Herself. Real.

Elisa came over and set the pale purple drinks down on the coffee table. Haven picked hers up and took a long slug. She'd already had two and they weren't working the way they needed to. "Get out the computer. Let's look at your database."

"Haven. That's not what you want."

"What does it matter what I want? It's over with Mark. He made it more than clear."

"Have you tried getting in touch with him?"

Not till you're ready. Not till you know what you want.

She kept hearing the way he'd described himself. *Burnout, has-been, drunk, brawler, scruffy unshaven guy with shit taste in clothes.* The way the world saw him, the way she'd seen him before she'd remade him. The way he believed she still saw him.

What she saw when she pictured him was the tenderness on his face when she'd told him how hard it was for her to get naked without making everything just so first. He'd said he didn't care if she was waxed or unwaxed, if her apartment was clean or dirty, he wanted her, and he wanted her to be comfortable.

"Haven," Elisa said patiently. "You are paying me a lot of money to fix your love life. A *lot.* And if you want that money not to be a total waste, I need to know what the hell is going on with Mark Webster. Aside from what the rags report, which is titillating and speculative but unsatisfying, I need you to tell me *everything*."

A tear ran down Haven's face. A single tear, which she swatted back like a bug.

"Oh, hon," said Elisa, and she scooted over on the couch and put her arms around Haven. "You *are* in love with him."

It all came out, then, all poured out, the whole story unfolding from beginning to end in its shameful beauty and chaos.

Charme, where Mark Webster had been his scruffy, combative self and Haven had not hated him nearly as much as she'd expected to.

The barbershop and the department store, Mark's unavoidable male beauty emerging from the layers of defense he'd piled over himself—the long hair, the shaggy almost beard, the awful clothes. And, as if it, too, had been hidden in there, his charm, the light in his eyes, the way he seemed to see through her—all the best of Mark rising to the surface.

The night at Village Blues, when she'd seen what all of that charm and light could do. When she'd seen inside him. When he'd gotten inside her.

The music lesson, when she'd understood how much he had to give to the world and she'd seen how deeply he cared about his father.

Their meeting with Pete in her office and their explosive encounter after he left. The way she'd tried to reduce what happened between them, to make it manageable. To put it in a box and tie it up neatly with a ribbon so it wouldn't break out and overwhelm her.

"You did *what*?" Elisa asked.

"It just *happened*," Haven said.

"Nothing *just happens* to you, Haven."

"This did." Her eyes filled up again. Her heart filled up again. The pain she'd been trying to hold at bay by not thinking about him threatened to burst out, like water held back by an aging levy.

Elisa was quiet so Haven went on with the story, and when she got to the dressing room in the department store, Elisa said, "No!"

"Yes."

"You didn't!"

"I did. And it was so, so good."

Because there was no longer any point in denying it. She could see, from where she was, that it had only been a matter of time until everything she felt would overwhelm her, when she would have to pay the piper for what she had denied. Eventually she would have to admit to herself and to Elisa what she had probably known from the first time her eyes had met Mark's in the barber shop mirror: that she loved him.

"And then what?"

"And then we went back to my apartment and had amazing sex. And then...and then I told him that we couldn't be together in public."

"Why?" Elisa asked.

"Because—"

But she didn't have the whole answer. She didn't know *how* to answer.

"Haven," Elisa said. "It's time for you to tell me about what happened with Porter Weir."

"I don't see what that has to do with —"

"Sweetheart. I don't even know the story and I know it has everything to do with this."

"We just—we weren't right for each other."

"I looked him up. Some people say he's gonna be the next poet laureate. Serious guy, huh?"

Haven's chest got tight, the way it almost always did when she thought about Porter Weir. "Not my usual type."

"Your usual type isn't your type, Haven."

"He was smart, deep, intellectual, angsty and emotional."

"And you were in love with him?"

"I was. Not like—" She couldn't quite say Mark's name and she couldn't quite link it together with that word, *love*. It hurt too much. But of course she didn't have to say it, because this was Elisa, and Haven could feel the leading edge of what, exactly, Elisa knew. That knowledge was building along with tears in her throat, pounding in her chest, tightness all the way to her fingers and toes.

"And then—?"

"He broke up with me."

Elisa didn't say anything. She didn't have to. She was perched on the edge of the couch, waiting patiently as if she had all day to hear Haven admit what she had held back from herself.

"He said that it didn't matter what I did. He'd tried everything he could to get me to open up, and he said that he knew I'd tried, too, but it wasn't something I could do. I'd spent too much time with surfaces. He said—"

Her voice disintegrated, but she held the splintered

bits together and managed to say it. "He said I was image all the way down."

Haven's heart beat hard and her stomach clenched around the hollow space that she'd envisioned inside herself ever since Porter had said that.

"Oh, hon," said Elisa, so kindly, so gently. "And that's what you've been so afraid of? That any guy who's worth anything will think you're image all the way down? Hav, you know that's not the truth, don't you, sweetheart?"

Something rose like a tide in Haven's chest, and her eyes welled with the held-back pressure.

"You're as real inside as that poet, hon. More real, because if anyone was a shallow asshole, he was."

Haven's laugh was almost a whimper.

"But Mark's not like that guy, right?" It wasn't quite a question the way Elisa said it, reassuring and even. "He already knows who you are and he hasn't run away."

That was what it took to break her down. Haven cried gallons of sloppy tears that required almost a whole box of tissues, which Elisa dispensed one by one until Haven subsided to small, ugly hiccups.

She looked at Elisa, who was sitting close, her face so sweetly sympathetic it made Haven want to start crying again.

"He hasn't run away," Haven agreed. "I did that for him."

"I WAS WONDERING when you'd show up here," Elisa Henderson told Mark.

"I looked you up on the internet."

"Glad to know my business is easy to find." She smiled at him. She was a tall, slim woman with gingerbread-colored hair. She possessed an overwhelming air of competence and the most sympathetic look in her greenish eyes. She leaned across her wide desk toward him and set her elbows on the surface as if settling in for a long story.

"Is this a conflict of interest?"

"No," said Elisa. "I often work with two halves of a couple. Sometimes two of my clients turn out to be perfect for each other, and it would be sheer foolishness not to get them together."

"But I'm not your client."

"Well," said Elisa. "I usually spend at least fifteen or twenty minutes talking to someone on the phone before they agree to sign a client agreement with me, and not all those conversations turn into business—although most of them do. So let's just pretend this is a phone call. You've got me for fifteen or twenty minutes."

"I don't—I don't even know why I'm here."

"Most people come because they want to find some-one."

That made a peculiar, deep pain slide down inside his torso, as though he'd swallowed something too big for his body. "Do they ever come and say, 'I found some-one but it didn't work out?'"

Elisa nodded. "Sometimes. Then usually I say, 'Are you sure you mean it didn't work out? Are you sure you don't mean *it hasn't worked out yet*?' Because most of the time, these things are a work in progress."

"I don't think it *can* work out."

"Tell me why not," Elisa said.

"I'm not the right guy for her."

"She tell you that?"

"Not in exactly those words, but yes—"

"Tell me why *you* think you're not the right guy for her."

"Just look at us," said Mark. "You've got Haven on one hand, totally put together, totally on top of things, beautiful, sexy, polished, dressed up, made up, hair up... and then you've got me."

Elisa shrugged. "Good-looking guy. Could use a shave. I'd lose that jacket—does anyone actually wear denim jackets? And those shoes look like they've seen better days."

"Seriously," Mark said. "Seriously, look at me and tell me you can see us together."

Elisa did exactly what he'd asked. She gave him a full-fledged, unrestrained, once-over. Before Haven had come along, getting such a look from a woman like Elisa would have been sexy, but now it felt as remote as an army sergeant's inspection.

"Okay," she said. "This is why you came here? So I could look at you and tell you to lose the jacket and buy a better pair of shoes?"

"No!"

"Then why?"

All at once he felt totally defeated. His head hurt because after he'd left the fund-raiser on Saturday night, he'd gone out and played blues and gotten stinking drunk, and he'd stayed stinking drunk for the better part of three days. His heart hurt now that he was sober, and he missed Haven in a way it hadn't occurred to him you could miss someone you'd known only a couple of weeks.

"I have no idea," he said. "I guess I wanted you to tell me I was wrong. I wanted you to tell me to fight for her, or—I don't know. I wanted some hope, I guess. When you look at us, do you see two people who can make things work? I guess I thought if anyone would know if it could work out, it would be you."

Elisa ran the pad of her thumb over the clip on a pen, a back and forth motion that was, somehow, soothing. She had a way about her, a professionalism, that he could see would inspire faith in her clients.

"No one knows if it's going to work out," Elisa said. "And when I look at you, I see two people who have whole entire worlds hidden inside them that I know nothing about. I can't do what you're asking. I can't look at the two of you, as if the answer is written on your skins, and say what will happen.

"I will say this. I think you're comparing your insides to her outside. People make that mistake all the time. You look at someone else and you think, I'm not good enough, I'm not worthy, they're so much more together than I am, or whatever you tell yourself. But you're comparing the mess on the inside to the neat and tidy package they present to the world.

"The real answer to the question is what happens when you finally stop trying to keep everything neat and just let the messes mingle. Do they add up to more than the sum of the parts? Here," she said. "Let me show you something. I don't think Haven would mind. Well, I'm sure she'd mind, but she'll forgive me someday." She turned her laptop around so he could see the screen. "Here are all the men I've fixed Hav up with." She began scrolling through them.

His first reaction was sheer envy. They were *those* men, those Don Dormers that Haven belonged with, neatly groomed, tidily dressed. He could see bits of their profiles rolling by, president of this and CEO of that, this big investment bank and that big corporation, well-known philanthropists. Men he wasn't. Men he couldn't be. Men he didn't want to be.

But when the screen kept scrolling up, he started to get what Elisa was telling him.

"How many?" he asked.

"I don't know. Twenty? Thirty?"

"And why doesn't it work out?"

"Different reasons. No chemistry, usually. They're boring. They're self-involved. She doesn't like their taste in ties. Never lasts past the second date, by the way. Make of that what you will."

No sex, Elisa meant. Twenty or thirty men who should have been perfect for Haven, and no sex.

She had never taken off her clothes for them. She had never taken down her hair or cleaned her apartment. She'd certainly never left it uncleaned because she was in a heated, hungry rush. And no one had to tell him that she had not jacked them in the backseat of a cab or let them lick her to orgasm in a dressing room.

She had never told them why those things were so hard for her.

She had never let them in.

He thought of how it had been at the fund-raiser.

He'd seen panic overtake her when Suellen had asked her for the truth and the way she'd covered it up with that peculiar expressionless face, the Haven mask. That was what had hurt the most, the lack of emotion. It had said to him that her public self was still in charge. She was still going to protect her image before her own heart—or his.

But over the past few days, he'd started to see it differently, started to hear her words, the ones she'd spoken on the curb, in his head. *Is that what you're afraid of?*

He saw now that he had answered Suellen for her, to keep her from having a chance to answer. He'd answered for her, just as she accused him, because he was afraid that she couldn't possibly want the man he really was.

Deep in his heart, he knew otherwise. She, of all people, *saw* who he was and had helped him find his way back to himself.

And he knew who she was. He knew her, and he knew that, as Elisa had said, for all the time she spent thinking about people's outsides, she spent at least as much thinking about their insides.

If he'd only given himself the chance, he could have helped her see her own insides as clearly as she saw his. He could still help her see that messy wasn't dangerous, that her mess plus his mess equaled something vastly greater than one plus one, that somewhere in all that chaos was truth and home and love. They could have something that would carry them as far as they needed to go.

"Mark," Elisa said.

He looked up from the screen. He'd been staring blankly at it for he wasn't sure how long.

"You aren't the man she thinks she wants."

"I know," he said.

"You're the man she knows she needs. That's not an easy job."

He closed his eyes for a moment. When he opened them, Elisa was regarding him with an expression of deep sympathy. "How do I fix things?" he asked her.

"Ah," she said. "To quote one of my favorite movies, 'I can only show you the door. You're the one who has to walk through it.'"

14

HAVEN TEXTED ELISA. I'm early. Send me pic so I can see if he's here?

Haven was sitting in Charme, waiting for her date. A week or so after she'd cried herself sick on Elisa's couch, her friend had emailed her to say she had a new match for Haven to try out. I think you'll like this guy, Elisa had written. He's your type.

Now Haven's phone buzzed in her lap, and she peeked toward the entrance of Charme again to see if she could spot a man who looked like he was in search of a blind date. Nothing. She read Elisa's text.

No pic. He has yours.

Elisa had been cagey about this guy from the start. She'd refused to show Haven his profile, saying that she thought it would cause Haven to "make assumptions" and "have expectations." Instead of giving Haven the guy's contact info, she'd made the plans herself—a late-ish dinner at Charme, followed by dessert at a new off-Broadway cafe that featured appetizers and sweets.

On paper, it sounded great, and Haven had dressed herself up obediently, putting up her hair, making up her face. But she had felt as if she was slogging through the process. There was no pleasure in any of it.

What she wanted to do was lounge on her couch and eat Cheetos.

If things had worked out with Mark...

Mark would sit on the couch with her and eat Cheetos. He would wear torn sweats and he would look hot as sin in them. He wouldn't care what she wore, either. She could wear one of his T-shirts and a pair of granny underpants and he'd think it was the sexiest thing on Earth. Maybe he'd do her up against one of the big street-facing windows of her apartment.

Heat—desire—flowed sweetly into her lower belly and welled in her sex. Tears filled her eyes. She had been the biggest idiot in three counties, and here she was, sitting and waiting for another of Elisa's dud guys to show up and bore her to death. She hated the too-tight foundation garment she wore under her uncomfortable dress, and the thong panties and the sharp pain in her scalp from where she'd pulled her hair too tight.

She removed a bobby pin, hoping to relieve the pressure, but somehow that made it worse. The weight of the twist now yanked harder on the spot that was too tight, and her head started to hurt. More tears flowed. In a moment her mascara was going to run right down her face, and when this new guy came into Charme looking for his date, he would find a crying raccoon.

Mark wouldn't care if she looked like a raccoon. He would just want her to be comfortable, as he'd said. She wouldn't have to worry about whether she was cheerful and put together and ready for this date. She could just come as herself.

She pulled another hairpin out. And then another. Her hair tumbled down onto her shoulders. She felt a tear slide down her face and knew it had painted a dark streak.

She crossed her arms, feeling defiant, though there was no one here to defy. She looked around the room as if daring anyone to give a shit that her hair was a collapsed, tangled heap or that her face wore twin stripes of misaligned war paint.

Then she realized who she was defying. Herself. Her own rules. She was telling that little voice in her—the one that was almost never silent, the one that constantly monitored the situation to make sure she was doing everything she could to *keep everything tidy*—to shut the hell up.

She didn't want to keep everything tidy. She was done with neat.

She could just come as herself.

She wanted to be her real, messy self, the one that cried in Charme and hurt—hurt like *hell*—because she didn't want to be here, she wanted to be with the one person in the world who had seen her lose control and hadn't turned away.

Who had seen inside her and wanted to stay a while.

She grabbed her phone out of her lap. Call it off, she

texted Elisa. Tell him I couldn't make it. Tell him horrible stomach flu.

What??? I can't do that now.

Please.

Her phone buzzed. Elisa, of course. Haven picked up the phone and hurried out to the sidewalk, answered Elisa's call with a swipe.

"He's on his way!" said Elisa, without preliminaries. "Haven, come on. Buck up."

"I don't want to do this." She was surprised at her own voice, flat and steely.

"Hav."

"I gotta go. I gotta go find Mark."

There was a long silence on the other end of the phone. "Haven, come on. Just stay put. Just do this for me. Just this one date. You'll be pleasantly surprised."

"Don't try to talk me out of this, Lise. I've been an idiot. I've gotta go talk to him. Right now."

Elisa made a sound Haven couldn't interpret. And she didn't care. It didn't matter any more if Mark was the right or the wrong guy for her on her paper, or whether Elisa thought she was stark raving mad. She didn't care if she looked crazy, if her hair was a nightmare, or if her makeup was streaked. Waving one hand she told Elisa, "I don't care how hot this guy is. Or how expensive his clothes are. Or how good his job is. Or how sexy his car is. Or how good he is at making small talk. Or how nicely his tux fits. I know I chose all those guys so they wouldn't reject me for being shallow. I know I broke up with them after one or two dates so they wouldn't have a chance to reject me. But I'm done. I don't want those guys anymore."

"Hav?" Elisa murmured, her voice as gentle as a feather settling in the grass. "It's okay, baby."

"Mark," said Haven, because she seemed to have used up all the words, and that was the only one that came out when she opened her mouth to speak again.

But Elisa seemed to understand. "Say it, Haven. You'll feel better."

Haven took a deep breath. Then forced it out through a throat tight with emotion. "I love him. I was sitting in there, and I realized I only want Mark. He might not want me any more. I was a jerk, but I have to try. I have to tell him. I have to give him a chance to see who I really am, and if it's not enough for him—"

"It's enough. It's more than enough."

That wasn't Elisa's voice. That was another, much deeper, very familiar voice, and it was coming from just above Haven. Slowly—so slowly, because she didn't want to discover she was hallucinating or dreaming or otherwise fabricating him straight out of thin air—she lifted her head, and there he was.

Mark.

Standing there.

Wearing a *very* nice suit.

Smiling down at her.

"Oh," said Haven. She blushed, because even though she'd meant every word she'd said, and even though she'd wanted him, passionately, to know it was all true, she would have presented it a little more…romantically…if she'd had time to think it through.

He didn't seem to mind, though. She didn't think she'd ever seen him smile that much, for so long, as if he was being lit up from inside. What a glorious smile he had. What a way of looking at her, like she was all that mattered, ratty hair and streaked face and all.

"Did he show up?" Elisa asked.

"Yes," said Haven.

"You'd better go, then," said Elisa.

"Yes," Haven repeated, and she didn't even try to find the right button to end the call, she just held down the off button on the phone and tossed it into her purse. And then she said, "You're my date."

"Yeah," he said.

"I was going to stand you up," she said. "Because I didn't think it was you. I thought it was another guy. And I didn't want another guy. I wanted you."

She seemed to be saying the most obvious things in the most obvious ways, but that didn't seem to bother him, so she kept talking.

"That would have been funny, I guess. In a missed-connections, hopefully-we-would-sort-it-out kind of way."

She felt as though the more she talked, the less she was saying what mattered, but again, he just nodded, and his smile grew a little.

"What were you going to do?" he asked.

"I hadn't gotten that far," she said. "I was going to find you. Wherever you were."

"And when you found me?"

"I was going to kiss you," she said.

"Like this?" he asked, and leaned down to press his mouth against hers.

"More like this," she said, and grabbed his head and really, seriously, kissed him, stroking his tongue with hers and biting his lower lip, feeling him already hard against her belly.

A car honked.

"They're saying we should get a dressing room," Haven said, and Mark laughed, a deep, unexpectedly rich and uninhibited sound.

"I went to see Elisa," Mark said, taking a step back from her but leaving his hands on her waist. "I needed to know how you felt about me. But then I realized I already knew. The problem was that I didn't know how *I* felt about me."

"You felt like you were a burned out, has-been, scruffy guy with shit taste in clothes," Haven said.

"Is that a verbatim quote?"

"Pretty much," she said. "I think I missed a few. I think you also said *drunk*."

"So I realized something," Mark said. "You helped me realize it, whether you know it or not. I *am* a burned out, has-been, scruffy guy with shit taste in clothes. Which is, like, the essential definition of a blues musician. I'm a blues musician. I'd just completely lost track during my years of Sliding Up, and then believing what Lyn said—"

She started to protest, but he said, "You were right. Lyn was wrong. And I was wrong to listen to her. I let her derail me for so long. I'm ashamed of how long."

"You were very young when she said that to you," Haven said gently. "And it was a very vulnerable moment. Things like that have a way of sticking."

He nodded. "Thank you. Thank you for saying she was wrong and making me look at myself again. And for making me hear myself again. I'm working on putting together a band—so I won't just do jams. I'll do gigs, too."

"That's great!" she said, and she couldn't help it, she grinned a huge dorky grin at him, and he grinned right back. "But I hope—"

He was already nodding. "And I'll be a music teacher. I owe you more thanks for bringing that back to me. I had twelve calls this week from new students, Hav, and I've already had to turn someone down because I just couldn't fit her into the schedule."

"Oh," she said, her heart too tight with emotion again to speak. But not panic this time. Joy.

"I'm not a pop star."

"No," she agreed.

"But I also realized that these are all costumes we put on. I *can* be a pop star for a few months, if that's what it takes to help my dad. I can go to fund-raisers and wear tuxes and give speeches. I can wear a suit and take you on a really romantic date."

"Yes," whispered Haven, feeling as if it was a superhuman effort to hold her whole body together and keep her feet on the ground, when she wanted to fly apart and float away. "And I realized—"

"That you can let your hair down and cry mascara streaks on your face, even in public?"

For some reason, that made her start to cry again, and he put his arms around her and held her while she got it all out of her system.

After a few minutes she was done, and she wiped mascara off her cheeks with the back of her hand, tidying up as best she could. Someone was going to show up any minute who knew her, and she was still Haven Hoyt. And Mark was okay with that. He would put on tuxes and suits and go where she needed to go and be who she needed him to be.

"I have an idea," she said.

"What's that?"

"Let's go on *both* our dates."

"How would we do that?"

"I will go to the bathroom and fix my hair and makeup," she said. "And we will go inside Charme and claim our table and eat. And then I will take you on your date."

"Okay," he said. "Where are we going on my date?"

"It's a surprise," she said.

He didn't mind Charme tonight. He didn't mind the pretentiousness of the decor or the schmoofiness of the food or the overbearing waitstaff. He sat across from Haven and looked into her big dark eyes and tried not to let his gaze get stuck in her cleavage, out of respect, even though it took a lot of willpower because that cleavage was a work of goddamned *art*.

She was telling him about her revelation, moments before the phone conversation he'd overheard, about not wanting to be with anyone but him. About the fact that he wanted her to "come as she was"—

"Hell, yeah," he said, huskily, and her eyes got darker and smokier, and her lips parted just enough to make his mouth go dry. Under the table, her leg slipped between his. The table was just big enough that they couldn't really get up to any mischief, which was okay with him, for now, because he had such a big, joyful sense of possibility. She was his tonight and tomorrow night and all the nights after that, in private and in public and wherever they went. He'd have plenty of time to get her messy.

"So I've been doing a lot of thinking, too," she continued. "I never felt like I fit in my family, growing up. They were women of substance—my mom and my sisters. They called me their princess, and I think maybe they even meant it affectionately, but I never took it that way. When I finally left home and started to be okay with who I was, I fell in love with this guy, this poet. He seemed like the kind of guy who would go for one of my sisters. Only he didn't, he went for me. And I thought, he thinks I have hidden depths. He thinks I'm not just a princess. But when he broke up with me, he said he'd never been able to get past my shell because there was nothing to get past. There was just more of the same, surface all the way down."

Oh, *hell* no, he *hadn't* said that to her. Mark wasn't sure what to feel right now, pain for the woman who'd listened to that bullshit and heard truth, or rage at the man who'd said those words to her. "Haven, *no*," he said. "He was *wrong*. Just plain *wrong*."

She smiled at him, a brave smile, the sweetest smile he'd ever seen, and the wonder of that swept away the other emotions and took root.

"What he said—it broke my heart. And I decided that I wasn't going to go after any more men who would hate that about me. I would find men like me, who wouldn't want to crack me open and then be angry when they didn't find what they were looking for."

"So that's why you dated all those—really boring guys?"

She laughed. "They would probably not be boring to *everyone*. They were just boring to *me*. And that's also why I never stayed with anyone long enough for him to get disappointed in me. When I heard you play music—God, you got straight under my skin. Into my blood. I admired it so much, the way you had all that passion and talent inside you. But I was pretty sure after a while you'd figure out there was nothing in me to match. I was pretty sure if I gave you long enough, you'd realize there was no substance to me."

He'd mistaken her hesitation for something to do with him, when all along it had been her, fighting herself.

She reached across the table and took his hand. For a moment she turned it palm up, as if she could read something there. Something about him, something about their future together. "When I was with you, I forgot that I was supposed to be guarding myself. And it was—well, to be honest, it was terrifying. And the deeper I got in, the more scared I was that you'd see the truth and run. That's what I was holding at bay. Not *you.* Not Mark Webster, blues musician, music teacher, all-around hottie, seriously smokin' lover. But I'm done. No more holding back."

"Haven Hoyt," he said. "You are not shallow. You are one of the least shallow women I know. Believe me. I've been peeling layers for weeks and I feel like I'm only starting to learn about the woman you are. You're intense. And loving. And passionate. Incredibly passionate. You see the world—and me—in a way no one else ever has. Not that I'm complaining about your surface," he said, giving her a heated look. He tried to fill that look with everything he planned to do with her later. Hopefully those activities would involve a certain pair of high-heeled sandals and a good leather belt. And the certainty that she'd be there when he woke up in the morning.

He watched her face flush and her pupils dilate and felt a deep sense of satisfaction—and peace.

There was a question he really wanted to know the answer to. *Needed* to know the answer to. "Did you mean what you said?" he asked. "What you told Elisa?"

She nodded. "I love you," she said.

It was strange. He'd known that truth already, known it intuitively, but hearing her say it out loud made such an overwhelming difference. Those words could awaken and transform, making him feel like a new man even when he already thought he'd done all the hard work of understanding who he was and who he wanted to be. His heart hurt, but a blissful kind of wide-open, broken-down, re-rendered pain. Glorious. "I love you, too," he said.

She smiled at him. Not her neat, tight, public smile, but a big, crooked smile, just for him.

It was easy after that. Easy to be with her, to listen as she told him she thought she'd get trained and maybe even certified in life coaching so she could help her clients do more of what she'd helped him do, to find his way beyond his image. He found it easy to fill her in on what he'd decided, where he would go from here. He'd do more music lessons, try to make that pay the bills. He'd play music, but just blues, no more wedding gigs, no more reunion tours once this one was over and the money banked to help his father with the move to New York. That should leave a sizable portion in savings, so even though being a music teacher wasn't the most lucrative job on Earth, he'd be able to support himself more than comfortably.

"Myself and—" He looked at her levelly. "Whoever else wants to tie their fortunes to mine."

"I might know someone who does."

"She might be a very welcome addition to my household."

"She might be very happy about that arrangement."

Her hands gripped his tight, and even though their words were casual, her eyes told him everything he needed to know. That there was nothing casual in her feelings, as there was nothing casual in his.

When they'd finished eating and paid their check, he said, "My turn, right?"

"Right," she said. "But you're overdressed for my date."

"I don't have anything else to wear."

"Come with me."

She made him walk with her back to her apartment and told him to wait while she ran upstairs. When she re-emerged into the lobby, she handed him a shopping bag from the department store where they'd made most of his clothing purchases the first day they'd shopped together.

He opened the bag and pulled out his old clothes— his ripped jeans, his grubby gray T-shirt, his bomber jacket.

"I was going to toss them," she said. "But I couldn't make myself do it. I loved them too much. I kept taking them out and…" She blushed. "I smelled them."

"Oh, yikes," he said. "Sorry about that."

"No," she said. "They smelled good. Like you. Leather and denim and soap and deodorant and okay, maybe a little bit of sweat."

"The sweat was because of the way you were looking at me in the mirror at the barbershop," he told her, which was totally true. "It's a miracle I didn't go up in flames."

"It's a miracle *I* didn't," she said.

"Where are you taking me?" he asked.

"On a messy date," she said.

And away they went, for ice cream that dripped on her dress, sticky cinnamon buns she had to lick off his fingers, and later, all the mess either of them could want, in Haven's apartment, which could use a cleaning, certainly, but neither of them could care less.

Epilogue

Eighteen months later

"HAND ME MY BRA."

"This is torture, you know."

"Just hand it over."

Mark reached down and found the lace bra where she'd tossed it on the floor of the limo. She stuffed it into her handbag, straightened her scoop-neck T-shirt, and asked, "How do I look?"

"Like you always look," he said. "Hot."

He was working fast, smoothing the pieces of his tux into the suit bag he'd spread out on the seat between them. Right now, he had his shirt off, and she took a moment to admire the view, lean muscle and just the right amount of hair.

"You know what we're like?" she asked. "We're like one of those movies, you know, something Bond, or *True Lies* or *Mr. & Mrs. Smith*, where they have the secret identities, and they're always changing fast in the back of some moving vehicle to become their other selves."

They were on their way from a celebrity's thirtieth birthday party—black tie—to a gig that Mark was playing at Village Blues. They'd both had to effect a complete costume change in the back of the car they'd hired to get them from one event to the other on time. And this wasn't the first time they'd done it.

"Except that everybody in New York City knows both of our identities," Mark said. Since they'd begun publicly dating, and since Sliding Up had officially announced its tour last year, the press hadn't given either of them much of a break. There had been photographs in the weeklies and online of the two of them together, at parties, at auctions, at fund-raisers, in blues clubs, backstage after Sliding Up concerts and emerging sweaty and red-faced from cabs, limos, department-store dressing rooms, back alleys and anywhere else they could grab a moment together.

There had also been some ugliness, yes, in the early days after the revelation that Mark Webster and Haven Hoyt were an item, plenty of speculation about whether Haven would destroy Mark the way Lyn had and how many of her clients Haven was intimate with. Also whether, perhaps, Mark and Pete were sharing Haven. When that gem had appeared in one of the weeklies, Haven had brought the magazine straight to Mark, because she knew they had to confront it, not hide from it. He'd taken the magazine from her, torn it into shreds, and then growled, *"I don't share."*

He'd provided a demo of how strongly he felt about that.

And then the buzz in the press had died down, and Haven's business had survived unscathed. In fact, her client list had grown as word got out that Haven offered life coaching to supplement her image consulting. The tour had only benefitted, as predicted, from the media madness.

Of course the media hadn't been remotely interested in the good news. No one reported on the fact that Mark's dad's move had gone smoothly, or that his health was improving more rapidly than predicted. It didn't make any front pages that he and Mark spent a lot of time shooting pool and even, occasionally, a basket or two. No one Tweeted that Mark was giving regular music lessons and helping Noteworthy with its fund-raising on an ongoing basis. And while Mark's band had been playing gigs sometimes four nights a week and had a solid following, it wasn't exactly a national story that he had been doing well enough that he'd turned down all the weddings they'd been asked to play.

Haven surveyed Mark, now clad in a clinging black T-shirt and his staple chewed-up jeans. "You know," she said. "I think I like you better this way."

"It's the holes in the jeans," he said, laughing. This particular pair, it was true, had some very attractive wear and tear. Haven privately thought Mark did it on purpose, but it was possible that his physique just put more than an average amount of strain on the denim.

The car pulled up in front of Village Blues, and they

emerged from the car, smoothly transformed into their blues-club selves. "Nice work," Haven said.

"One of these days," Mark said, his voice growly, "I'm going to jump you when your clothes are off, and we're never going to make it to the next stop at all."

"Is that a promise or threat?" Haven inquired.

"A threat," Mark confirmed, and Haven felt her heart speed up as it always did when Mark displayed his alpha side.

In the club, she found a table for four. She watched Mark get ready and begin warming up. Warming *her* up, that was. His hand slid up and down the neck of the guitar and she planned what, exactly, she was going to do to him later that night.

She heard her name called out, and looked up to see Elisa and Brett hurrying toward her. Elisa gave her a huge hug, and Brett kissed her on the cheek, and the four of them settled down and ordered drinks. And enormous slices of chocolate cake, in Elisa's and Haven's cases. The only thing hungrier than Elisa's eyes when her cake arrived were Brett's, watching Elisa put the cake away. He'd been on a business trip the past week, Elisa had told Haven, so they couldn't promise to stay till the end of the night.

Haven took a bite of her cake. "Oh, my God, this is good."

Mark's gravelly voice crackled through the mic. "Thanks so much for coming out tonight. Most of you guys know this is my new band, Mark and the Real Men. I want to start out with a special song tonight.

Those of you who know me at all know I don't write music and I don't sing, but I made an exception in this case."

Haven's face got hot.

"I wrote this song for a woman who taught me how to put it on, how to take it off and, most of all, how to be real."

She was going to cry. She was going to sit here with tears streaming down her face in front of everyone and—

And she didn't care at all. Maybe she even liked it a little. Because this was what it felt like to have your insides on the outside. It hurt in exactly this beautiful way.

"Haven, sweetheart, I love you so much."

She wrapped her arms around herself, hugging, and he smiled and pointed at her and blew her a kiss.

Mark used that mysterious brand of hand signals that looked like magic to Haven, getting the band playing, slow and sexy. And then he sang his song to her.

She knew the blues now, the way the meaning hid in the coarse words. She knew there was often no romance, no prettiness. Sometimes it was all sex on the surface, and sometimes it was something else completely on the surface and sex all the way down. She was okay with that—with all of it. Because she knew how sex was sometimes the first way you could say what you needed to say, sometimes before you even knew what it was you wanted to say. As if your heart spoke a language that was somewhere between body and soul, and the only way to bridge the gap was to acknowledge the messy reality of being human.

Baby put away your broom
And put away your wet mop
No need to clean up or look your best
I like when you're a hot mess

Baby put away the pricy shoes
And forget the fancy hairdo
No need to buy that thousand dollar dress
I like when you're a hot mess

Floor's clean enough to eat off of
You look good enough to eat, too
No need to pass any kind of test
I like when you're a hot mess

When he was done, when the last note faded away
and the room flooded with applause, she ran up on stage
and let him enfold her in his arms, let them take their
pictures, run their video cameras, capture the moment.
They would see what was on the outside, and inside—
she was alight, alive, in love.

* * * * *

COMING NEXT MONTH FROM

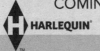 **HARLEQUIN®**

 *Blaze*

Available January 20, 2015

#831 A SEAL'S SECRET
Uniformly Hot!
by Tawny Weber
Navy SEAL Mitch Donovan is used to dangerous missions.
But working with Olivia Kane on a Navy-sanctioned fitness
video has him on high alert. It will take all his skills to survive
his encounters with the red-hot trainer!

#832 THE PERFECT INDULGENCE
by Isabel Sharpe
Driven New Yorker Christine Meyer and her mellow California
twin sister agree to swap coasts and coffee shops—to
perk things up! Tall, extra-hot (and sexy) Zac Arnette wants
everything on the menu...including the steamy Chris!

#833 ROCK SOLID
by Samantha Hunter
Hannah Morgan wants to trade her good-girl status for a
smoldering adventure, just as bad-boy race-car driver
Brody Palmer is trying to change his image... Will he change
his mind instead?

#834 LET THEM TALK
Encounters
by Susanna Carr
3 sizzling stories in 1!
Inspired by some illicit reading, three women shock their small
town when they tempt the sexy men of their dreams into joining
in their every fantasy...

HBCNM0115

REQUEST YOUR FREE BOOKS!
2 FREE NOVELS PLUS 2 FREE GIFTS!

HARLEQUIN®

Blaze®

red-hot reads!

YES! Please send me 2 FREE Harlequin® Blaze™ novels and my 2 FREE gifts (gifts are worth about $10). After receiving them, if I don't wish to receive any more books, I can return the shipping statement marked "cancel." If I don't cancel, I will receive 4 brand-new novels every month and be billed just $4.74 per book in the U.S. or $4.96 per book in Canada. That's a savings of at least 14% off the cover price. It's quite a bargain. Shipping and handling is just 50¢ per book in the U.S. and 75¢ per book in Canada.* I understand that accepting the 2 free books and gifts places me under no obligation to buy anything. I can always return a shipment and cancel at any time. Even if I never buy another book, the two free books and gifts are mine to keep forever.

150/350 HDN F4WC

Name	(PLEASE PRINT)

Address		Apt. #

City	State/Prov.	Zip/Postal Code

Signature (if under 18, a parent or guardian must sign)

Mail to the **Harlequin® Reader Service:**
IN U.S.A.: P.O. Box 1867, Buffalo, NY 14240-1867
IN CANADA: P.O. Box 609, Fort Erie, Ontario L2A 5X3

Want to try two free books from another line?
Call 1-800-873-8635 or visit www.ReaderService.com.

* Terms and prices subject to change without notice. Prices do not include applicable taxes. Sales tax applicable in N.Y. Canadian residents will be charged applicable taxes. Offer not valid in Quebec. This offer is limited to one order per household. Not valid for current subscribers to Harlequin Blaze books. All orders subject to credit approval. Credit or debit balances in a customer's account(s) may be offset by any other outstanding balance owed by or to the customer. Please allow 4 to 6 weeks for delivery. Offer available while quantities last.

> **Your Privacy**—The Harlequin® Reader Service is committed to protecting your privacy. Our Privacy Policy is available online at www.ReaderService.com or upon request from the Harlequin Reader Service.
>
> We make a portion of our mailing list available to reputable third parties that offer products we believe may interest you. If you prefer that we not exchange your name with third parties, or if you wish to clarify or modify your communication preferences, please visit us at www.ReaderService.com/consumerchoice or write to us at Harlequin Reader Service Preference Service, P.O. Box 9062, Buffalo, NY 14269. Include your complete name and address.

HB13R2

Halloween

"My, oh, my, talk about temptation. A room filled with sexy SEALs, an abundance of alcohol and deliciously fattening food."

Olivia Kane cast an appreciative look around Olive Oyl's, the funky bar that catered to the local naval base and locals alike. She loved the view of the various temptations, even though she knew she wouldn't be indulging in any.

Not that she didn't want to.

She'd love nothing more than to dive into an oversize margarita and chow down on a plate of fully loaded nachos. But her career hinged on her body being in prime condition, so she'd long ago learned to resist empty calories.

And the sexy sailors?

Livi barely kept from pouting. She was pretty sure a wild bout with a yummy military hunk would do amazing things for her body, too.

It wasn't willpower that kept her from indulging in that particular temptation, though. It was shyness, pure and simple.

But it was Halloween—time for make-believe. And tonight, she was going to pretend she was the kind of woman who had the nerve to hit on a sailor, throw caution to the wind and do wildly sexy things without caring about tomorrow.

"My, oh, my," her friend Tessa murmured. "Now there's a treat I wouldn't mind showing a trick or two."

Livi mentally echoed that with a purr.

Oh, my, indeed.

The room was filled with men, all so gorgeous that they blurred into a yummy candy store in Livi's mind. It was a good night when a woman could choose between a gladiator, a kilted highlander and a bare-chested fireman.

But Livi only had eyes for the superhero.

Deep in conversation with another guy, he might be sitting in the corner, but he still seemed in command of the entire room. He had that power vibe.

And he was a superhottie.

His hair was as black as midnight and brought to mind all sorts of fun things to do at that hour. The supershort cut accentuated the shape of his face with its sharp cheekbones and strong jawline. His eyes were light, but she couldn't tell the color from here. Livi wet her suddenly dry lips and forced her gaze lower, wondering if the rest of him lived up to the promise of that gorgeous face.

Who is this sexy SEAL and what secrets is he hiding? Find out in A SEAL'S SECRET by Tawny Weber.
Available February 2015 wherever Harlequin® Blaze books and ebooks are sold!

JUST CAN'T GET ENOUGH
ROMANCE
Looking for more?

Harlequin has everything from contemporary, passionate and heartwarming to suspenseful and inspirational stories.

Whatever your mood, we have a romance just for you!

Connect with us to find your next great read, special offers and more.

Facebook.com/HarlequinBooks
Twitter.com/HarlequinBooks
HarlequinBlog.com
Harlequin.com/Newsletters

HARLEQUIN®

 A Romance FOR EVERY MOOD™

www.Harlequin.com